Muluk Chand

The Trial of Muluk Chand for the Murder of His Own Child

A Romance of Criminal Administration in Bengal

Muluk Chand

The Trial of Muluk Chand for the Murder of His Own Child
A Romance of Criminal Administration in Bengal

ISBN/EAN: 9783337007775

Printed in Europe, USA, Canada, Australia, Japan

Cover: Foto ©Andreas Hilbeck / pixelio.de

More available books at **www.hansebooks.com**

THE TRIAL

OF

MULUK CHAND

FOR

THE MURDER OF HIS OWN CHILD.

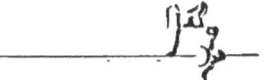

A ROMANCE

OF

CRIMINAL ADMINISTRATION IN BENGAL.

WITH AN INTRODUCTION

BY

W. A. HUNTER, LL.D., M.P.

London:
T. FISHER UNWIN,
26 PATERNOSTER SQUARE.
1888.

INTRODUCTION.

THIS report of the strange case of Muluk Chand, a humble watchman in a small village of rural Bengal, is published from the original record, with a narrative from the pen of Mr. Manomohan Ghose, who acted as counsel to the accused on the second trial. Besides the interest that always attaches to the great dramas of life when played out on the stage of the criminal courts, there are instructive points in the case as illustrating some of the characteristic features in the administration of English and Indian criminal law.

Muluk Chand was convicted unanimously by a jury for the murder of his daughter, aged 9 years. The principal witness against him was a younger daughter, aged 7 years, who stated that she had seen the murder committed. The Sessions Judge, Mr. P. D. Dickens, a "competition *wallah*," was as fully convinced of the guilt of the accused as of the truth of the proposition that "two and two make four". But the capital sentence cannot in India be executed when a Sessions Judge pronounces condemnation until it is confirmed by the High Court. Some of the persons who heard the trial were not convinced of the justice of the verdict, and a subscription was raised for the purpose of engaging counsel when the case came before the High Court. After a lengthened debate, Mr. M. Ghose convinced two judges that there was sufficient doubt to justify them in ordering a new trial. Upon the second trial the accused was acquitted, as it appeared almost certain that no murder had in fact been perpetrated. The mode in which the deceased met her death was not disclosed to counsel until after the verdict was given on the second trial.

An English lawyer cannot help being impressed with the superiority, in one respect, of criminal procedure in India. Had the case occurred in England, the only appeal would have been to the Home Secretary, and he would have been compelled to arrive at truth without the aids that a public trial affords. The High Court in Calcutta is a more suitable tribunal to consider appeals; and the manner in which this Court discharges its duties has caused it to be regarded with veneration by the people of India as the noblest manifestation of British justice.

The light that this case throws upon the administration of justice in the rural districts of Bengal is somewhat painful. The miscarriage of justice was due to the corruption of the police and their determination to support a wrong opinion by tutoring a child in falsehoods to swear away its father's life. At the same time the readiness of the people to perjure themselves is a fact full of significance as to the difficulty of carrying out a pure administration of the law.

A candid study of the facts in this case will inspire grave doubts of the expediency of certain changes in English criminal procedure that have been adopted in India. In England the evidence of the three women who stated that the little girl told them what she had seen on the morning of the murder would not have been admissible. Mr. Dickens admitted it under the provisions of Section 157 of the Indian Evidence Act, which is to the effect that any statement made by a witness, at or about the time when the fact to which it relates took place, is admissible in order to corroborate the witness.

Such a rule gives enormous scope to perjury, and enables a prosecution to multiply witnesses. It gives a false appearance of corroboration, and in this case undoubtedly led to a fearful miscarriage of justice. Evidently the experiment of altering the rules of evidence has in this instance proved a failure.

It is a singular fact that the whole case for the prosecution against Muluk Chand would have collapsed if the Sessions Judge had exercised a power that he possessed of calling for the production of the police papers. The practice in India is to enter in a diary at the police office, noting the day and hour, every fact and statement made concerning a police inquiry.* So much importance does the Indian law attach to such statements, that any person wilfully making a false statement to the police is exposed to the punishment of perjury, just as if he had made the statement as a witness at the trial.† The accused parties have no right to inspect the police records—it is difficult to see why—but the Judge may call for them and examine them himself. Had Mr. Dickens done so, he would have found an entry showing that the police had dug up the floor of Muluk Chand's house, searching for the snake which was supposed to have killed the girl. A perusal of the trial shows that this fact is totally inconsistent with the theory of the prosecution ; and if Mr. Dickens had laid his finger on it, the whole edifice of perjury would have fallen to the ground.

* Section 172 of the Indian Criminal Procedure (Act X. of 1882) enacts :—
" Every police-officer making an investigation under this chapter shall day by day enter his proceedings in the investigation in a diary, setting forth the time at which the information reached him, the time at which he began and closed his investigation, the place or places visited by him, and a statement of the circumstances ascertained through his investigation.

" Any Criminal Court may send for the police diaries of a case under inquiry or trial in such Court, and may use such diaries, not as evidence in the case, but to aid it in such inquiry or trial. Neither the accused nor his agents shall be entitled to call for such diaries, nor shall he or they be entitled to see them, merely because they are referred to by the Court ; but if they are used by the police-officer who made them to refresh his memory, or if the Court uses them for the purpose of contradicting such police-officer, the provisions of the Indian Evidence Act, 1872, Section 161 or Section 145, as the case may be, shall apply."

† By Section 161 of the Indian Criminal Procedure Code every person is " bound to answer truly all questions relating to the case put to him by the investigating police-officer other than questions the answers to which would have a tendency to expose him to a criminal charge or to a penalty or forfeiture," and under the Indian Penal Code, any person who, being under a legal obligation to tell the truth, makes any statement which he knows to be false or does not believe to be true, commits the offence of perjury.

I

At the second trial both the native doctor who made the *post-mortem* examination of the deceased girl and his European superior were present and were cross-examined. It was elicited on this cross-examination that the wound, from which the girl was supposed to have died, was more probably inflicted after death. But the singular thing is that the attendance of these medical men was not compulsory.* Indeed, medical witnesses do not usually appear at the trial when they have been examined before the committing magistrate. Considering that, at the first stage, prisoners are usually without legal advice and no cross-examination can take place, this practice is full of danger. It may be that there are great demands upon the time of medical officers in India, but nothing can justify the practice of receiving evidence which has not been tested by cross-examination, and upon which at the trial no cross-examination can take place. The Judge has a discretionary power to compel the attendance of medical witnesses at the trial, but this is hardly a matter that ought to be left to the discretion of the Judge. A prisoner has a right that no testimony should be admitted at the trial unless his counsel has an opportunity of testing its value.

Except in providing a proper Court of Criminal Appeal, it would appear that the innovations in criminal procedure that have been introduced in India, so far as this case throws light upon them, are not calculated to further the ends of justice.

W. A. HUNTER.

---

* Section 509 of the Indian Criminal Procedure enacts :—

" The deposition of a civil surgeon or other medical witness, taken and attested by a magistrate in the presence of the accused, may be given in evidence in any inquiry, trial, or other proceeding under this code, although the deponent is not called as a witness.

" The Court may, if it thinks fit, summon and examine such deponent as to the subject-matter of his deposition."

TRIAL

OF

MULUK CHAND CHAUKIDAR.

CHAPTER I.

RECORD OF THE FIRST TRIAL.

NUDDEA SESSIONS COURT.—May 16, 1882.

(Before P. D. Dickens, Esq., Judge.)

THE EMPRESS *v.* MULUK CHAND CHAUKIDAR.

THIS case was committed by the Deputy-Magistrate of Bongong, in the district of Nuddea in Bengal, and tried by the Sessions Court. The prisoner was charged with having, on the night of the 27th March, 1882, murdered his own daughter, Nekjan, aged 9 years, with a view to bring a false charge of murder against one Kadam Ali Fakir. The Jury having found the prisoner guilty, the Judge, who concurred in the verdict, sentenced the prisoner to death, subject to confirmation by the High Court. The evidence recorded by the Judge at the trial consisted of the following depositions:

The deposition of GOLAK MANI, aged about 7 years:—

[The child was first questioned by the Foreman of the Jury, and gave intelligent answers, and said that to tell a falsehood was a sin. She was then affirmed in the usual way.]

I remember my sister—my elder sister. Her name was Nekjan. She is dead. She died on our verandah. It was night. My father killed her.

This is my father. [Points out prisoner.] " I myself saw him do it. He first put his foot on her throat, and afterwards struck her (*mariachilo*) on the body [points to a spot just below the abdomen] with a spear. My sister did not cry out. I was awake. Something touched my body and woke me. I was in the verandah. I said— "*Baba, maritecho kano ?*" (" Father, why are you killing ? ") He said nothing. I was afraid. It was then not dark (*pharsha*). After this my father told me that I was not to tell the *daroga* (police inspector) if he came, and that I was not to tell my mother when she came back. She had gone the evening before to Goga. My sister Nekjan gave me my meal that night. Next morning Dhiru gave me my meal. I told Dhiru in the morning, and my mother and Haru. Haru came first to the house very early in the morning, and I told her first, and then Dhiru came and I told her, and told my mother when she came.

After my father struck my sister I did not go to sleep. My father after that cried, and I cried. After killing my sister my father went out, and returned some time afterwards.

I stayed where I was. I did not think of going out and telling my aunt then. This is the spear—our spear. My father had been sleeping on the same mat (*bichana*) my sister and I were sleeping on, before my sister was killed. When I spoke to Haru first I was in the compound. I was sent to the field by my father on the next day. I did not see the *daroga* send away the body. I did not see the body taken away. I was sent to the field early in the morning after my meal.

My father had treated me more kindly than he treated my sister; but he used not to treat her unkindly.

I knew my sister was dead, because she did not answer me, and when I tried to rouse her by pulling her body, she did not move.

To Jury.—My father began to cry when he came back in the morning.

To Prisoner.—No one has tutored me. I have spoken the truth.

[*Note by the Judge.*—This little child gave her evidence intelligently, and in a way which impressed me with a belief that she had witnessed the scene she described, and was not repeating a story learned by rote.]

(Sd:)   P. DICKENS.

Witness No. 2.,

Deposition of ADHAR CHANDRA CHAKRAVARTI, aged about 35 years, taken on solemn affirmation under the provisions of Act X. of 1873, before me, P. Dickens, Esq., Sessions Judge of Nuddea, the 16th day of May, 1882 :—

My name is Adhar Chandra Chakravarti. My father's name is Ramkumar Chakravarti. I am by caste Brahmin. I reside at present in Mouza Bongong, where I am Civil Hospital Assistant, in charge of Bongong Sub-Division.

I examined the body of a girl identified to me as the body of Nekjan by Dwarika, constable, on the evening of the 29th March, Wednesday, about 4 P.M.

Decomposition was setting in on the scalp, but not on the body.

I made a *post-mortem* examination, and have drawn out a report. This is the report [marked Ex. A. put in and read].

When I say the mouth was closed and the tongue protruded, I mean that the teeth had closed on the tongue, which was protruding.

The protrusion of the tongue and the congestion of the eyes are signs of strangulation.

I did not suspect strangulation, and therefore made no examination under the skin to see if there were marks of pressure under the skin of the throat.

The wound on the loin was sufficient to cause death. The wound was a gaping wound, *i.e.*, the lips of the wound had not closed. It was a wound visible to anybody looking at the corpse. I see this spear. The wound I speak of could have been caused by this spear. The child was not a healthy child. Her liver was enlarged.

To Court,—There was a *sari* (cloth) on the body up to the waist. No blood whatever on it. There were signs of internal bleeding. None of snake-bite.

(Sd.)   P. DICKENS.

POST-MORTEM REPORT, EX. A.

HOUR OF DESPATCH.	HOUR OF EXAMINATION.	INFORMATION FURNISHED BY THE POLICE.
29th March, 1882, at 10 A.M.	29th March, 1882, at 4½ P.M.	Death by snake-bite. Deceased's father could not give any information regarding the death. An incised wound of a triangular form, measuring about one finger, was found on the epigastric region.

CONDITION OF SUBJECT.	WOUNDS.	BRUISES.
Emaciated.	One punctured wound resembling the character of an incised wound on the epigastric region measuring one inch long, ¼ inch broad, and about ½ inch deep; this wound has penetrated into the convex surface of the left lobe of the liver about ¼ inch deep; there was also one scratch mark about 2 inches long, ¼ inch broad, on left cheek.	None.

MARK OF LIGATURE ON NECK.	SCALP, SKULL, AND VERTEBRÆ.	
None.	Scalp neatly decomposed, skull and vertebræ healthy.	

MEMBRANES.	Duramater slightly congested.
BRAIN AND SPINAL CORD.	Brain congested.
PLEURA.	Healthy.
PERICORDIUM.	Healthy.
WALLS, RIBS, AND CARTILAGE.	Healthy.
DISEASE.	Liver little enlarged.
LARYNX AND TRACHEA.	Healthy.
LUNGS.	Slightly congested.
HEART.	Both ventricles empty.
VESSELS.	Healthy.
SMALL INTESTINES.	Healthy.
FRACTURE.	None.
DISLOCATION.	None.
PERITONEUM.	Slightly congested.
MOUTH, PHARYNX, AND ÆSOPHAGUS.	Healthy.
STOMACH.	Healthy and empty.
LARGE INTESTINES.	Healthy.
LIVER.	Little enlarged and congested. Punctured wound ¼ inch deep.
SPLEEN.	Slightly congested.
BLADDER.	Healthy and empty.
ORGANS OF GENERATION.	Healthy.
	Healthy and empty.
	Healthy.

Mouth shut up, tongue swollen, enlarged and protruded; eyes congested; frothy blood came out from the nostrils; one scratch mark on the left cheek, 2 inches long, ¼ inch broad; and one punctured wound on the epigastric region measuring about one inch long, ¼ inch broad and about ½ inch deep. This has penetrated into the convex surface of the left lobe of the liver about ¼ inch deep. About 3 ounces of liquid blood was found on the abdominal cavity.

I am of opinion that the deceased met with her death by the penetrating wound of the abdomen.

(Sd.)   A. C. CHAKRAVARTI,

Civil Hospital Assistant, Bongong.

The wound in the abdomen was probably the cause of death.

(Sd.)   J. BRANDER,

Civil Surgeon.

Witness No. 3.

Deposition of RAMDAS SIRKAR, aged about 30 years, taken on solemn affirmation :—

My father's name is Joychand Sirkar. I am by caste Kayast. My house is at Mouzah Sarsa, where I am a head-constable of police.

I am in charge of Sarsa Thanna (police station). I was in charge on the 27th of March last. I received information of this murder on the 28th March (Tuesday) at about 3½ P.M.

The information was given by the accused.* He brought no written information.

To Court.—It is customary to bring a written information in cases of murder.

I took down his statement in writing correctly. This is not it. [*Note by the Judge.*—The first *izahar* (information) is not with the record, and I cannot admit secondary evidence of its contents.]

The prisoner after making his *izahar* (statement) went home. I followed, and arrived at the village at 7½ A.M. on the morning of the 29th March. I saw the body of a child. It was lying in the verandah of the house of Muluk Chand, the prisoner. The body was then

---

* The information given by the accused was to the effect that on his return home that morning from his field, at about 4 A.M., he found his child dead in bed, and that he did not know the cause of death.

lying on its back. The legs were not doubled or drawn up, but stretched out. The arms were straight and by the side of the corpse. It was lying on a mat. I saw no blood-stain at all on the mat.

The verandah showed no signs of having been freshly *leped* (wiped) or cleaned.

I saw a wound—the edges were not closed but open., No blood was coming out. The accused was there.

The *punchayet* (village headman) was there, and the prisoner's wife was there. I did not see Golak Chokri (girl) there.' The prisoner said he could not tell how she had come by her death.

The prisoner's wife did not then make any statement to me. I made this map. It is correct as a rough map, though not drawn to scale. I did not see Golak Mani all that day (the 29th).

The next day I was at the *thanna* (police station). I made no attempt at investigation on that day, the 29th. I took down only the statement of the prisoner in writing. I did not take down the statement of the wife in writing. She told me nothing about the murder. I made the map on the 31st March, when I returned with the inspector who investigated the case.

To Jury.—The *thanna* (station) is nine miles from the village. I forwarded the body on the 29th March in Dwarik's charge. I did not see the spear or this *bagi* (sword) the first day I went there. I enquired for no weapons that day. I can't say why I went away from the village without making further report in the case. I made a written report that day. This is it. [Ex. C.]

Having made this inquest report, I returned without making any enquiry into the crime. I first began to investigate that on the 31st, when I went on with the inspector.

(Sd.)   P. DICKENS.

Witness No. 4.

The deposition of BARAHTI, aged about 25 years, taken on solemn affirmation :—

My father's name is Khodabux, Mussulman. My house is at Mouzah Bhulat; where I was living with my husband.

The accused is my husband. I had a daughter named Nekjan. She is dead. She was about 8 or so., She was older than Golak. I had a little son aged 2½. The night that Nekjan died I was not in my house. I had gone to Goga. My husband had sent me to Goga the evening before. He first told me to go about midday, and I started in the evening about a *danda* (24 minutes) before sunset. I was told to fetch money from his brother, Gopal, to meet the expenses of a case brought against him by Fakir. I got no money. I returned next day about four *danda* or so in the morning, the time the cows are taken to the field. I heard cries. My child Golak was crying, and my husband was also crying. I saw the body of Nekjan lying in the verandah. I saw a hole in the body just above the abdomen. The wound was not bleeding. It looked dry. I questioned the accused, saying—"How has this happened?" He said—"I went to look after my onions, and don't know how she was killed". I said—"I have no quarrel with anyone; who has done this? No one has done it but you." I did say—"Is this why you sent me to Goga?" He said—"Think about the means of escape". I then asked the little girl, and she told me in answer to my questions that her father had put his foot on the child's neck, and (*maria-phelya*) after she was killed thrust the spear into her.

I believed the girl's statement, and I said to him—"I won't give you rice any more with my own hand," to which he made the answer—"*Tomar hatai bhat amar ar khaetai hoeba na*".* After that I cooked no food for him. I did not notice the spear then. I see this spear. [Produced.] It is my husband's. He has one spear only. This weapon (*bagi*) is also his. They were usually kept in the thatch of the verandah. The *daroga* (police officer) came next day. I did not see the *daroga*. He asked me no question. He came to the house, but I was in a different verandah from the verandah the corpse was in, and I was not brought before the *daroga*. He did not ask me any question that day. I was first questioned two days afterwards by the other *daroga* (inspector), and I told him what I have told the Court.

I can't say why I did not tell the *daroga* the first day and denounce my husband. It was not from fear. I had my children, and I had not seen the act myself, and I was not asked.

I had taken the two youngest children with me to Goga, because the youngest was at the breast, and the elder cried, and I could not leave her alone.

There was a case pending against my husband. Fakir had

* "I shall not have to eat rice from your hands any more."

brought that case. He was the complainant, and it was about his wife.

To Jury.—Before this I was on good terms with my husband, and he treated me kindly.

[*Note by the Judge.*—This witness gave her evidence freely and without any apparent wish to make any points against her husband, and without any display of animus against him.]

(Sd.)   P. DICKENS.

16th May, 1882.

Witness No. 5.

Deposition of HARU, aged 40 years :—

I am living with my son. My husband is just dead. I remember a morning—a Tuesday morning—about two months ago, hearing of Nekjan's death. My house is about two or three *rushis* (80 or 120 yards) from the prisoner's house. This is Muluk Chand. He was the father of Nekjan. That morning I went to his house he was crying, and a little girl, Golak, was crying. It was then quite light (broad day), but the sun had not risen. I heard no cries (calls), but merely sobs. I saw Muluk Chand sitting in the verandah and the little girl. I saw Nekjan's body in the verandah. I went close to the verandah, and stood and looked at the body.

I did not go up the stairs into the verandah.

To Court.—The body was lying on its back. The legs and arms were stretched out, not drawn up. I asked Golak what had happened. She said—" My father put his foot on her throat and thrust his spear into her ". My child then began to cry, and I had to go. I had left her at home. I did not question Muluk Chand. I then saw that the dead child had a wound above the abdomen. I saw no blood about. When the child Golak told me this, her father got up and threatened her, saying—" If you say this I will put my foot on your throat ".

Then I went away. I saw the *daroga* (police officer) come next day. I did not tell him that day, but two days afterwards.

[*Note by the Judge.*—I admit this statement under Section 157, Ev. Act.]

Witness No. 6.

The deposition of DHIRU, aged about 40 years, taken on solemn affirmation, 16th of May :—

My father's name is Khoda Bux. I am by caste Mahomedan. My home is at Mouza Bhulat, where I am living with my husband.

I knew Nekjan, Muluk Chand, prisoner, was her father. My house is about one *rushi* (40 yards) off his. I remember her death. It took place about two months ago. Next morning early I heard Muluk Chand crying. I went there. Golak was sitting near the corpse. I saw the body of Nekjan in the verandah, but I did not look carefully. I asked the little girl, but she said nothing then. Muluk Chand said nothing then. I went back home, and shortly afterwards I called the little girl to my house, to take her food. About a *prahar* after sunrise (9 A.M.) I questioned the child, saying—" You were sleeping with your sister ? How did she die ? " She said the *baba* (father) put his foot on her neck and killed her. She did not then mention the spear. I suspected then the father. Her mother was not then at home. She came at bathing time. I did not see her, however, that day. I did not go near the house that day again. I know nothing more.

To Jury.—I can't say why the father did such a deed. He treated her well before this.

(Sd.)   P. DICKENS.

Witness No. 7.

The deposition of UMA CHARAN SIRCAR, aged about 40 years, taken on oath or solemn affirmation, under the provisions of Act X. of 1873, before me, P. Dickens, Sessions Judge of Nuddea, this 16th day of May, 1882 :—

My name is Uma Charan Sircar. My father's name is Bangsidhar Sircar. I am by caste Kopali. My home is at Mouza Bhulat. I am a *punchayet* and cultivator.

I know the accused. He is the *chaukidar* (watchman), of my village. I knew Nekjan, his daughter. On the 16th *Chaitra* (28th March) last I got some information from Umesh Ghazi, in consequence of which I went to the house of accused. Accused was there. I got to the house about four *dandas* after sunrise (7 A.M.). I saw the body of Nekjan in the verandah, covered by cloth. I saw no blood on the cloth or on the mat. I did not go into the verandah. I looked from outside. I questioned Muluk Chand as to the wound I saw on the chest above the abdomen. He said he could not say who had caused that wound. I saw this spear lying in the road five or 'seven *hâths* (3 or 4 yards) from the verandah, and I saw this *bagi* lying close to a blacksmith's shop—four *bigahs* (160 yards) from the verandah. I asked why the spear and *bagi* were out there, and he said he didn't know. He said they were both his. I said—" Leave the things exactly where they were, and go and give information to the police ". I gave him no written *ittala* (notice). I said I would write one, but he went without coming to me for it. I did not see either Golak or the mother when I went to the house. I did not then ask anyone else. I suspected the prisoner somewhat because of his weapons lying about. He told me he thought she must have died from snake-bite.

To Court.—This was after I saw the wound.

(Sd.)   P. DICKENS.

Recalled.—The man Fakir, who has brought a criminal charge against accused, is living in the same village.

(Sd.)   P. DICKENS,
Sessions Judge.

Witness No. 8.

The deposition of Dr. BRANDER, aged about — years, taken on oath before me, P. Dickens, Sessions Judge of Nuddea, this 16th day of May, 1882 :—

I am Civil Surgeon of Nuddea. I have read and considered this *post-mortem* report. The appearances, recorded by the examiner, are consistent with death having been caused by the spear wound. A wound one inch deep would puncture the liver, and cause death, but not in my opinion immediate death necessarily ; but it might cause immediate death by shock. If a man of the weight of the accused were to put his foot on the neck of a slight child, it would be sufficient to cause death. The pressure alone would cause death, by suffocation. I should say death was caused immediately by the wound, but there is nothing inconsistent with strangulation and partial suffocation. As a rule, bayonet or spear wounds do leave a convulsed appearance on the body, but if strangulation was taking place, or had taken place, the body would not have the vital energy to develop the position which is characteristic of the death caused solely by spear-wounds.

I can explain the absence of blood externally in this way, that if the death was owing to a mixed cause, by suffocation and the thrust, the arterial system would have become partially inactive as the result of the suffocation, and would not have caused the expulsion of blood to a distance, which would have been the case if the spear-wound alone had been the cause of death. This may also be explained by internal bleeding. The ventricles of the heart are reported empty. Bleeding, therefore, must have supervened. It may have been internal.

To Jury.—If the edges of the wound were gaping, the wound must have been caused before life was wholly extinct.

(Sd.)   P. Dickens.

Ex. D.

EXAMINATION OF THE ACCUSED PERSON.

The examination of Muluk Chand Chaukidar, aged about 35 years, taken before me, Gopal Chandra Mukerji, Deputy-Magistrate, 1st class, at Bongong, on the 31st day of March, 1882 :—

My name is Muluk Chand Chaukidar. My father's name is Ashruf Sirdar. I am by caste Mahomedan, and by occupation *chaukidar.* My home is at Mouza Bhulat.

Q.—Did you murder your daughter Nekjan?

A.—No, I did not kill her.

Q.—On what date, and when did she die?

A.—Early on Tuesday I went to look after my onion field ; no one was in the house except the two girl ; my wife had gone to Goga on Monday afternoon. On my return from the field I saw my eldest daughter, Nekjan, lying at a little distance from her bed. I called her, but she did not answer. I felt her body, but she did not move. When it was daylight I saw that she had a wound, and was dead, and my daughter, Golak Jan, was asleep. I began to cry. At four or six *dandas* of the day (8 A.M.) I was going to the *thanna*, . when I was arrested by a *piada* (peon) on the complaint of Kadam Ali Fakir, who had taken out a warrant against me.

Q.—After that, when did you go to the *thanna* ?

A.—After midday I went to the *thanna* and informed the *daroga* (police inspector).

Q.—How far is the *thanna* from your house ?

A.—Four or four-and-a-half *kos* (8 or 9 miles).

Q.—When did you leave your daughters and go to the field ?

A.—When there was one *prahar* of the night remaining (3 A.M.).

Q.—Why did you send your wife away from your house ?

A.—To obtain money, with a view to defray the expenses of the case that was pending against me.

Q.—Is this spear yours?

A.—Yes.

Q.—Why does it look as if it had been rubbed ?

A.—I cannot say, I did not rub it.   I did not take it with me to the field.   I took my *latti* (stick).

Q.—When you go to the field or to your watch do you carry the spear or the *latti* ?

A.—Sometimes I take the spear, sometimes I take the *latti* (stick).

Q.—Whom do you suspect having killed your daughter?

A.—I did not see anyone killing her, and my suspicion does not fall on anyone; but I have a quarrel with Kadam Ali Fakir and Mirun.

Q.—How many spears have you got ?

A.—Only this one ; the other one has been falsely produced as mine.

Q.—Had your daughter any ornaments on her person ?

A.—No.

EXAMINATION OF THE ACCUSED.

Under Section 346 of the Criminal Procedure Code, by Mr. Dickens, Sessions Judge of Nuddea, dated the 16th May, 1882.

My name is Muluk Chand Chaukidar.   My father's name Ashruf Chaukidar ; by caste, Mussulman ; inhabitant of Goga, Thanna Sharsha, at present residing at Bhulat.

Q.—Are you guilty of the charge ?

A.—I am not guilty.

Q.—Did you make this statement before the Deputy-Magistrate, and is it correct ? [Read, exhibit D.]

A.—Yes, I made this statement, and it is correct.

Q.—Why did you send your wife to Gagan,.instead of going there yourself ?

A.—Lest the police should find me absent from the village and beat me ; through fear of this, I did not go.

Q.—Why did you not go during the day ?

A.—They (my people at Goga) do not stay at home during the

day, but go out to the field, &c., and cannot be found at home' during the day, so I did not go during the day.

Q.—You have said that you saw, on your return from the field at night, that your daughter was lying at some distance from her bed, and that you called the neighbours at daybreak. Why did you not light a lamp as soon as you came and saw, and why did you not immediately call your neighbours instead of keeping quiet?

A.—I called out for my neighbours as soon as I saw my child on my return from the field.

Q.— Did you tell the *punichayet* of the village and the police at the *thanna* that your daughter had died of snake-bite?

A.—Yes, I said that my neighbours say that my child has died of snake-bite.

Q.—Will you call any witnesses?

A.—Yes, I will.

Q.—What will they say?

A.—They will say that they said about the snake-bite.

P. DICKENS,
Sessions Judge.

[The prisoner called three neighbours as witnesses for the defence, and these men said they knew nothing as to how the child died, but that they had heard a report in the village to the effect that she had died from snake-bite.]

THE JUDGE'S CHARGE TO THE JURY.

GENTLEMEN OF THE JURY,—The prisoner is charged with murdering his own child, a little girl of 9 years of age. There is no question of law on which I need detain you. If you find that the prisoner has committed the act with which he stands charged, it will be your duty to return a verdict of guilty of murder under section 302, Penal Code. The question which you, gentlemen, have to try, then, is a question of pure fact: Did the prisoner really kill his daughter, as alleged?

The prisoner in his defence has relied on the *primâ facie* want of motive: Why should I have killed my daughter? The motive alleged is, that the prisoner was at enmity with one Kadam Ali Fakir, who had brought a criminal charge against him (whether for adultery or taking his wife away is not shown); that criminal proceedings were imminent; and that either to implicate his enemy or to save himself and stave off further proceedings, he murdered his own child. The motive briefly would, therefore, be 'partly revenge, partly self-preserva- tion. It is proved beyond doubt that criminal proceedings were impending on the 27th March. Now, the enormity of the offence charged must not be allowed by you to obscure your judgment in dealing with the evidence as to its commission. Neither should you allow the apparent weakness of the motive, in comparison with the magnitude of the crime, to obscure your judgment. The prosecution cannot, of course, be answerable for the former, and with regard to the latter, it is my duty to direct you that the prosecution is not bound to prove the motive. It is sufficient if they prove beyond reasonable doubt that the prisoner committed the act. [A passage from the charge of Campbell, C.J., in Reg. v. Palmer, quoted at page 44, Wills on Evidence, fourth edition, was here read.] Now, the prose- cution have indicated a motive, and have shown that there was pressure of immediate difficulties. He had to meet a serious criminal charge, and had no funds in hand to meet it with. The adequacy of the motive is no doubt a matter for your consideration. But it is not a point which the prosecution is legally—that is, as a matter of law—bound to prove.

It lies on the prosecution, firstly, to prove by the medical evidence that the crime of murder was committed; and, secondly, to establish in your minds a reasonable belief, amounting to a moral certainty, that the prisoner committed that crime. It is their duty to prove these two points by the best evidence which the nature of the case admits. If, by the best evidence which the case is capable of, they induce this degree of belief in your minds, such a conviction, that is, as you would each act upon in the gravest affairs of your own lives, you must not hesitate in doing your duty on speculative doubts as to the adequacy of the motive. It is, no doubt, an atrocious and violently improbable act for a father to kill his own child. But it is a still more atrocious and violently improbable act for a man's wife and child and neighbours to compass his death by deliberately perjured testimony. You are face to face with two violent improbabilities, one of which, according to the laws of thought, must be true. Either the child is speaking truly or not : if she is, her father is guilty ; if she is not, she has been suborned to take away her father's life by deliberate falsehood. And her mother, her aunt, and her neighbours have voluntarily joined this conspiracy. Whichever hypothesis you adopt, a shock is given to ordinary experience and ordinary probability, and yet it is absolutely certain that one must be true.

Atrocity for atrocity—apart from any evidence, you are asked to accept the lesser.

But you are bound to decide the issue of the prisoner's innocence or guilt on the evidence before you. Leaving, therefore, mere speculation as to conflicting probabilities and the inscrutable mystery of motive, it is your duty to examine the direct evidence in this case, and to see if it is consistent with all the other facts of the case—with medical evidence and with the circumstantial evidence. You must test the truth of the direct evidence, that is, the girl Golak's evidence, in every possible way by these external tests, and you should also test it by the internal touchstone of demeanour. If the way in which the child gave her testimony has impressed you favourably ; if you can come to the conclusion that the manner of her narrative was that of an eye-witness and not of a child repeating a lesson ; if you find her testimony corroborated by the other witnesses, under Section 157, Evidence Act, and borne out by the medical evidence, and by the circumstances on which the prosecution relies as inculpatory facts—then the direct evidence of the child is legally sufficient for conviction. It is sufficient in law, and, if corroborated to your satisfaction, you should have no hesitation in convicting upon it.

I say, if corroborated, because though, legally, corroboration is not needed, I could not advise you to accept the evidence of a child of that age unless it was very strongly corroborated. A child of six or seven, especially in this country, is unquestionably of sufficient intelligence to narrate truly and distinctly what she has really seen. The theory for the defence, in fact, tacitly admits that the child is a competent witness, for on that theory she is a perjured and suborned witness. If she is intellectually capable of giving an absolutely false description of a scene she never witnessed, in a manner sufficiently natural and life-like to deceive educated and experienced gentlemen like yourselves, she is, *a fortiori*, capable of describing events of which she was an actual spectator. The theory, then, that she is a tutored witness destroys and cuts away the arguments that she is an incompetent witness. For my own part, I have formed, in the course of a somewhat lengthy criminal experience, a very high opinion of the capacity of young children in India to relate vividly what they have actually seen, provided, of course, that the facts are of sufficient importance to impress themselves on their memory. You, gentlemen, however, are sole judges of facts in this case, and you must not take my opinion on this point as a direction on the degree of weight you should attach to her evidence.

[The evidence of Golak was here read.]

Having laid this girl's evidence before you, I now propose to go through the other evidence, and to indicate the matter for your decision on the following points :—

(1) Whether the medical evidence supports the girl's testimony on important particulars ;

(2) Whether the rest of the direct oral evidence supports the girl's statements ;

(3) Whether the circumstantial evidence, especially the conduct of the prisoner, corroborates it or not.

[The evidence of Dr. Brander was here read.]

Now, this evidence, and what you have heard from the native doctor, very distinctly corroborate the girl's story as to the manner of her sister's death, that is, the double nature of the means employed, as to what Dr. Brander calls the mixed character of the cause of death. The absence of blood is a peculiar feature as to which all the witnesses agree. It is, of course, possible that some blood-stains may have been removed by the prisoner before the body was first seen; but the medical evidence appears to account sufficiently for the absence, by concomitant or antecedent strangulation coupled with internal bleeding. The position of the body and the position of the wound on the apex of the abdomen point also to internal bleeding. But the absence of blood externally, and the very slight depth of the wound, are, it appears to me, important corroboration of the child's statements. If the child was not killed by the prisoner, the murder must have been committed by an outsider and an enemy. The child wore no ornaments. An outsider, if intending to murder, and using a spear to effect his purpose, would, in all probability, have struck home, that is, deeply, and withdrawn the spear quickly, in which case there would have been two things: (1) a discharge of blood, and (2) a deeper wound. Whereas if death were caused really by a heavy man's foot upon the throat, if suffocation had partially or completely supervened, if the spear had been inserted deliberately and slightly, not to kill, but to give a colour to the theory of murder by an outsider, and slowly withdrawn, the admitted circumstances of the absence of blood-stains and the shallowness of the wound are satisfactorily explained. Here, then, in the scientific testimony, which is above suspicion, is a species of corroboration which could not have been foreseen by the concoctors of a fabricated story.

"I now come to the direct oral testimony which is adduced to corroborate the truth of the girl's story.

[Evidence of Haru, Dhiru, Bahrati, was here laid before the Jury.]

These witnesses all agree in saying that the girl told them the same story on the morning of the 28th March, and before the police came near the village.

If they are speaking the truth, these facts afford the strongest possible corroboration of that story. If the child has been suborned, they also must have been suborned to support her. It is for you to weigh this body of evidence, and to come to a conclusion for yourselves as to whether it is trustworthy. There is a discrepancy between the evidence of-Haru and the girl as to the place where the statement was made. The child says that it was in the *utan* (yard), the woman says that it was in the verandah, the child was sitting. But that is very trifling, for the woman at all events was in the *utan*, and it does not appear to be a point to which much importance should be attached. I shall have to comment further on the mother's evidence, but for the present I will leave it, and come to the third branch of the evidence—the circumstances which the prosecution relies on as inculpatory.

And first as to the spear. The spear produced is admitted by the prisoner to be his, and there seems no reason to doubt that the murder, whoever committed it, was committed with that spear. If not, why (on the hypothesis of the prisoner's innocence) was it left lying outside for the *punchayet* to see ? Taking it, then, to be the spear or weapon with which the murder was committed, whoever committed it, which theory best accords with ordinary experience and reasonable probability—the child's story that the supposed murderer used his own spear, or the theory that an outsider used the prisoner's spear ? That the night was dark is an admitted fact. It is proved that the spear was usually kept in the thatch of the verandah, a place where the darkness of the night would be intensified. When a person comes in the darkness of the night to commit a deliberate murder on a neighbour's child, does he come empty-handed ? Does he not usually come with some instrument—a club, a *dao*, or a spear—to accomplish his design ? The theory for the defence would require the outsiders to have come empty-handed, or not to have used the weapon they brought. Again, looking at the fact that the place where the spear was kept was in the thatch, the outsider was either a man familiar with the house or he was not. If *not*, it is extremely unlikely that he would have found the spear in the dark; if *yes*, it is extremely unlikely that he would have come empty-handed, relying on finding the spear. The prisoner says he usually took the spear when absent at night, and an outsider must, if intending murder, have counted on his absence. As far as it goes, then, the weapon used corroborates the child's story. The prisoner unquestionably had the weapon with which death was inflicted, and it is improbable that any outside murderer would have come intending to use that weapon, and unprovided with a weapon of his own. I would not advise you to attach excessive importance to this point if it stood alone, but it is, as far as it goes, corroborative. In coming to a conclusion as to the truth of the girl's evidence—in other words, as to the prisoner's guilt or innocence, the conduct of the prisoner himself becomes an element of the utmost importance—a test, under the peculiar circumstances of the case, of the highest value. What was his conduct before the event ?—at the time of the event ?—after the event ? Was it on the whole consistent with the conduct of an innocent man in his position ? Was it consistent with the conduct of a man against whom, on the hypothesis of innocence, an abominable crime had been committed ? These are important questions for you, gentlemen, and on your answers to these questions, it is plain, much will depend. It is for you to decide what answers you will give to these questions, and what effect these answers will have on the conclusion to which you may come on the whole case. I will merely point out the bearing of the evidence on these points.

First,—What was the conduct of the prisoner before the event? He sends his wife away the evening before, so as to ensure her absence during the night; for what ostensible purpose ? To fetch money (which was not forthcoming) from his own brother. Not from her relatives, be it remarked—from his brother. The village Goga is within an easy distance—half-an-hour's walk or twenty minutes' run for a strong and tall man like the prisoner. And yet he does not go himself, but sends his wife. You have seen that sending his wife entailed her taking the two youngest children, and disturbing the ordinary household arrangements. You have heard the prisoner's explanation of this act, and it is for you to decide whether it is a sufficient or satisfactory explanation. Such an act, even if altogether unexplained, is not, of course, inconsistent with innocence, and if it stood alone, could not, of course, support a legal inference of guilt. But if, in your opinion, insufficiently explained, it is a circumstance which adds to the cumulative force of the inculpatory facts—a circumstance corroborative of the theory for the prosecution.

Second,—What was the conduct of the prisoner at the time of the event, *i.e.*, on the night of the murder? [Prisoner's statement before the Magistrate read.] He comes home in the dark; he finds his child, on his own showing, dead. He strikes no light. He gives no alarm. He does not (on the hypothesis of innocence) *then* know what is the matter with her. It may be snake-bite; it may be a sudden seizure of illness. What would a man ordinarily do under such circumstances? Would he not get a light, and call his neighbours? The aunt of the girl, the sister of the man's absent wife, is living within hail, yet the prisoner admittedly does not summon her to his help. He waits till it is light, and then examines, and sees a death-wound on his child's body. Even then he gives no alarm. He calls no one. He begins to wail and weep in such a way that his neighbours, then astir, hear it and come to inquire. Far be it from me to say that his weeping at seeing his child lying murdered—were he an innocent man—would be improbable or unnatural. But on his own showing the outburst of sorrow did not come till the break of day, and the question is whether his conduct antecedent to the outburst of sorrow, real or pretended, is compatible with the conduct of an innocent man. The woman Haru swears it was broad daylight when she went. Why up to that time had the prisoner called no one to his help? If help was past, why had he called no one to witness the abominable crime, the foul murder that had been perpetrated in his house? You have seen that in his statement to the Magistrate he distinctly said that he came home in the dark, and did not see the wound till the dawn came. He could not, if that statement be true (and it was admittedly made

and correctly recorded), have known that help was past. When asked
to explain his conduct by me, he sees the importance of the inference,
and attempts to contrádict his former statement—whether satisfactorily
or not is for you to judge.

Third,—What is his conduct after the event? His position
compels him to report the death. He knowe an inquiry must follow.
Does he take proper steps to report the real facts, to place the magni-'
tude of the crime in the true light, to insist on justice being done on
the unknown murderer? No, he tries to stifle the inquiry by report-
ing at the *thanna* that the neighbours say it is a case of snake-bite.
The written information has unfortunately not been sent up, as it ought
to have been, by the Deputy-Magistrate, and I have accordingly been
unable to admit secondary evidence of its contents. But the *post-
mortem* report shows that the case was reported in the first instance
as a case of snake-bite, and the prisoner has admitted before you that
on going to the *thanna* he mentioned that the neighbours said it was
a case of snake-bite. He has called three witnesses, telling you that
they would prove this statement. Here, therefore, is no *bonâ fide*
and straightforward charge of murder made in the first instance by an
outraged parent. An attempt to stifle inquiry is made by a false repre-
sentation. But, it may be asked, does not this at all events cut away the
ground from under the feet of the prosecution? Does it not clearly
show that the prisoner had no *animus* against Kadam Ali? Does not
the alleged motive, the object of the prisoner's alleged act, the founda-
tion of the case, fail? At first sight, gentlemen, it does. There, is
no doubt a complete change of front. But if you examine the evidence carefully, the reason will be apparent. If Haru's evidence be
true; the prisoner knew that he could not shut his child's mouth.
Before the sun rose his own child had declared him to be a murderer.
His *coup* had failed before the *punchayet* came ; he must have felt (if
his child's evidence be true, and if Haru's evidence, be true), that it
was hopeless to carry out his intentions—that in attempting to strike
down his enemy he would involve himself in ruin, and that his only
chance of safety lay in burking the inquiry., On that hypothesis

alone can the statements to the *punchayet* about a snake-bite—can the statements at the *thanna* about a snake-bite, be explained consistently with either hypothesis. If innocent, and if his child had not denounced him, why persist in such a preposterous explanation, with a ghastly death-wound staring him in the face and giving him the lie? If guilty, and if his child has denounced him, they become explicable. He may have argued that the police, hearing the neighbours say that it was a case of snake-bite, might not have taken the trouble to inquire. When the police did come, and an inquiry became inevitable, did he do what lay in his power to further the inquiry and to bring the murderer to justice? [The evidence of the head-constable was here laid before the Jury.] This man, on his own evidence, appears to be unfit for his duty. On his own showing, he made no sort of inquiry into the crime which the evidence of his own senses must have shown him had been committed. He examined no one but the father, the present accused, and left the village on the 29th March, the day he arrived, without attempting to make any proper investigation. His explanation is that he was only holding an inquest, and was awaiting the native doctor's report before beginning an inquiry. This conduct, however absurd, does not affect the main question before you, one way or the other. It only goes to show that the prisoner did not press an inquiry upon him, and did not produce his daughter, Golak, on the 29th March. That, as far as it goes, if you believe the witness's statements, tends to support the theory for the prosecution, and to corroborate the important statement of the girl that she was sent away to the neighbouring field on the 29th March. That statement, if you believe it, is a strong inculpatory circumstance, for Golak was the only person who was in the house when the murder was committed,-and, on the hypothesis of the prisoner's innocence, should have been produced before the police officer, who had come to the village to make an inquiry.

That, gentlemen, concludes the case for the prosecution. It is only on the mother's evidence that I can find a single circumstance of importance that appears to throw doubt on the story as told by the prosecution — that circumstance is her omission to denounce her husband to the head-constable on the 29th March. This is her explanation of the omission. [Read.] It is for you to weigh that circumstance and the explanation given. It may be that she was on that day unwilling to denounce her husband, or uncertain as to the course she ought to pursue. It may be that she was unwilling to cut away her means of support. It may be that she was overcome with the fear of her husband, and doubtful of the result of a direct accusation coming from her. She may have felt that she would be unable to substantiate that accusation. She says, " I had not seen the act myself," and she may reasonably have felt that the girl's evidence might be insufficient to bring her husband to justice. Her failure would have exposed her to his revenge and lasting enmity. All these considerations may have been operating in her mind, and have prevented her taking it upon herself to make a formal charge on her own responsibility.

It is for you to weigh these matters, and to attach what weight you think fit to the circumstance that the prisoner has not rebutted the case made by the prosecution in any way, should you think that the case is established on the evidence. He has called three neighbours to prove, as he says, that the villagers talked about snake-bite as the cause of death before he went to the *thanna*, and agreed that that was the cause of death. The witnesses called certainly do not prove or bear out that allegation. Even if they did, it is difficult to see how it would tend to prove the innocence of the accused, except on the hypothesis that he is devoid of natural intelligence. Snakes, when they bite, do not make holes in a human being's body, and the wound on his child's person must have been a fact patent to his senses. With these observations, I shall leave this case to you. If the evidence for the prosecution does not satisfy you of the prisoner's guilt, if you have reasonable doubts of the truth of the child's evidence and the sufficiency of the corroboration, you should acquit the prisoner. If, on the other hand, you find no room for reasonable doubt, if your minds are convinced by the whole evidence that the prisoner committed the act which caused death, you will not be doing your duty as citizens if you shrink from convicting the accused of murder.

(Sd.)   P. DICKENS,

Sessions Judge.

VERDICT AND SENTENCE.

The Jury are unanimous in finding the prisoner guilty of the offence specified in the charge, viz., that he committed murder, an offence punishable under Sec. 302 of the Indian Penal Code, and the Court directs that, subject to confirmation by the High Court, Muluk Chand Chaukidar be hanged by the neck till he is dead.

[When the Judge passed sentence of death on the prisoner, and informed him that if he wished to appeal to the High Court, he must do so within seven days, he said that his last prayer was that he might be hanged in his own village, where there were persons who would feel that he was being unjustly hanged for a crime which he had never committed.]

CHAPTER II.

THE PRISONER'S APPEAL

TO THE HIGH COURT OF CALCUTTA, JUNE, 1882.

(Before the Honble. Mr. Justice Wilson and the Honble.

Mr. Justice Macpherson.)

CAPITAL SENTENCE CASE.

THE EMPRESS *v.* MULUK CHAND, CHAUKIDAR.

MR. MANOMOHAN GHOSE, who appeared for the prisoner, said :— This case, my Lords, has been referred by the Sessions Judge of Nuddea, for confirmation of the sentence of death passed by him upon the prisoner, and it also comes before your Lordships on an appeal preferred by the condemned man, on whose behalf I appear. It is a case of unusual difficulty, whether looked at from the point of view of the prosecution or from that of the defence. The prisoner has been found guilty by the unanimous verdict of a Jury, consisting of his own countrymen, of the atrocious crime of murdering his own child, a girl of 9 years, of whom, according to the evidence, he was very fond, and the motive ascribed by the prosecution for this crime, which renders it even more inhuman, is that the prisoner intended to fix the guilt of the crime upon an enemy of his, Kadam Ali Fakir, with whom he had been on bad terms. Ordinarily, where a Jury have unanimously found a prisoner guilty, it becomes exceedingly difficult to induce this Court to interfere with the conviction; and although, in capital cases, the law allows this Court to examine the evidence and disturb the verdict of a Jury even on questions of fact, yet in the present instance the prisoner's appeal would, at first sight, seem to be desperately hopeless, by reason of the witnesses in the Court below not having been at all cross-examined, with the exception of one solitary question to one witness put by the prisoner himself, who was undefended. Besides this apparently almost insurmountable difficulty, the prisoner stands condemned on the evidence of an eye-witness who is no other than his own child, corroborated by the evidence of his own wife. Nevertheless, the case presents many features of so startling a character, that I venture to think your Lordships will hesitate to confirm the sentence of death passed by the Lower Court, even if you are unable to declare the prisoner absolutely innocent, on a perusal of the record now before you.

In trials by Jury, a prisoner under sentence of death appealing to this Court is in a much better position than any other who has received a lighter sentence; for in the latter case no appeal lies except on a point of law, while in capital cases the Legislature has wisely enabled this Court to examine for itself the evidence adduced before the Jury, and to form its own opinion upon the value of that evidence. The first point arising on the evidence in the case, which I shall submit for your Lordships' consideration, is the total absence of motive for so inhuman a crime. It is true, as the Judge in the Court below remarks, that the prosecution is not bound to prove any motive as a matter of law, but in considering the value of the evidence and the probabilities of the case, regard must be had to the adequacy of the motive suggested for the crime. And what is the motive suggested here by the prosecution? To bring a false charge of murder against an enemy. Although crimes of that kind are not altogether unknown in Bengal, yet the Courts will require very strong evidence before coming to the conclusion that a man has killed his own child for the purpose of having his revenge upon an enemy by accusing him falsely of murder. In this case, happily, the prisoner's own conduct entirely negatives any such theory.

[*Wilson, J.*—Whom did the prisoner accuse?]

He never accused anyone, and never even said that his child had been killed. His statement to the police from the beginning has been—" I don't know how my child died; my neighbours imagine she died of snake-bite ". But the prosecution suggests that the prisoner must have changed his mind shortly after the murder, and therefore never ventured to charge Kadam Ali Fakir. It is difficult to understand why he should have changed his mind if he had killed his daughter for the sole purpose of accusing the Fakir. As regards the prisoner's motive, then, the suggestion of the prosecution is wholly unwarrantable. The Judge, in his charge to the Jury, has throughout assumed that the case must be one of deliberate murder, and has on that hypothesis asked them to adopt one of two alternatives presented to them, viz., either the prisoner murdered the child, or some enemy of his committed the crime. This was a very serious mistake ; for the case clearly admits of another hypothesis, which never suggested itself to anyone in the Court below, but which has made a very great impression on my mind since I first read the evidence, and which it will be my duty to ask your Lord- ships to adopt in this case. The Judge's charge to the Jury is an elaborate, a laboured, and, I may be permitted to add, a very able effort at persuading them to come to one conclusion, and one con- clusion *only* in the case. He has given the Jury no chance of avoid- ing the conclusion at which he had himself arrived, viz., that the prisoner committed the murder. Such a charge must have necessarily prejudiced the prisoner, and it would entitle me to ask your Lord- ships to interfere on the ground of misdirection, even if it were not open to your Lordships to review the evidence in the case.

[*Wilson, J.*—But there is the direct evidence of the prisoner's own child, who was not cross-examined. How are we to disregard that evidence?]

In dealing with the evidence of the child, your Lordships must have regard, in such a case as this, to probabilities, and remember that the prisoner, an ignorant peasant, would be absolutely incompetent to cross-examine any witness himself. No doubt *primâ facie* the evidence of a child is regarded as more reliable than that of an adult; but in this country it is notorious that advantage is frequently taken by the police and others of the precocity of Indian children, who are easily tutored to give false evidence which the most skilful cross-examination sometimes fails to expose. In this case, when your Lordships consider the improbability of the story told by the child, and the other evidence in the case, I feel confident you will come to the conclusion that no reliance ought to be placed on her testimony. To my mind, the very fact that the child is giving her evidence against her father, and the wife against her husband, is almost itself sufficient to indicate that they are witnesses who have been put up for the occasion to tell a particular story, and that there is some mystery at the bottom of the case which the evidence does not disclose.

[The whole of the evidence was then read and commented upon.]

Mr. Ghose then proceeded:—It is of the utmost importance in cases of this description to notice when and how the accusation was originally made. If the child Golak had actually seen her father kill her sister, it is utterly inconceivable that, when the head-constable went to the prisoner's house on the 29th, the prisoner was not denounced as the murderer by anyone. This is perhaps the most important part of the case. How was it that neither the neighbours nor the prisoner's wife accused the prisoner on the 29th March? The head-constable swears that the prisoner's wife was questioned by him, but she said nothing. She, however, falsely denies having been asked at all by him. This is a contradiction upon a very important point. If the wife wished to screen her husband then, what was it that led her to accuse him subsequently? The fact is beyond all doubt that the prisoner was never accused before the police until after the result of the *post-mortem* examination was known. And this is a clear indication that the police put pressure upon the child and the wife, and made them tell the present story after the doctor had declared that it was not a case of snake-bite. I would submit with confidence that in this country this circumstance alone renders the evidence absolutely worthless, although the witnesses have not been cross-examined. It is notorious that the police in this country wait for the result of the *post-mortem* examination, and then proceed to manufacture evidence so that it may fit in with the medical evidence. The story told by the child clearly shows that this is exactly what was done on the present occasion.

[*Wilson, J.*—But how do you account for the death of the child? It was not a case of snake-bite.]

It is not absolutely necessary that the prisoner should be able to account satisfactorily for the death of the child, if he had nothing to do with it. But in the present case I can put forward a theory which suggested itself to me the moment I read the papers of the case, and which furnishes, in my judgment, the real clue to this mystery. Anyone who has any experience of criminal trials in Bengal knows that in the vast majority of cases, probably in more than 90 per cent., neither the prosecution nor the defence discloses the whole truth. There is always, unfortunately, a desperate attempt on both sides to conceal the facts as much as possible, and our Courts have therefore the very difficult task imposed upon them of finding out, as best they can, the truth out of an immense mass of false and perjured testimony. Bearing this in mind, also remembering that ignorant persons in this country when accused of crimes will not tell the truth, and will set up a false defence even though they are absolutely innocent of any crime, I have little hesitation in saying that, after the most anxious consideration of the whole evidence, I have come to the conclusion that this was a case of accidental death.

[*Wilson, J.*—The medical evidence shows that death was caused by the wound in the abdomen which penetrated the liver.]

I shall ask your Lordships to reject the medical evidence on that point. I cannot conceive of any such wound having been inflicted during life, and yet not a drop of blood coming out of it. The child's clothes and bedding had no blood on them.

[*Wilson, J.*—How do you say the accident was caused?]

In the absence of any information, I can only speculate. Is it altogether unlikely that the prisoner, who was sleeping on the floor of his verandah with his daughters, had occasion to get up during the darkness of the night, and happened to tread on the throat or chest of the deceased? I do not say that this is a satisfactory explanation, but it is a possible one.-

[*Wilson, J.*—But supposing such an accident had killed the child, how do you account for the wound?]

My Lords, the wound presents no difficulty whatever to me, and it is because I am able to account satisfactorily for the wound that I ask your Lordships to hold that the death of the child must have been due to some accident. Appearing for the prisoner, it is no doubt a very dangerous suggestion for me to make, but knowing the character and the ideas of these ignorant people in Bengal, I venture to assert that this wound was made after death.

[*Wilson, J.*—Who made it, and why?]

It was probably made by the prisoner himself to account for the death of the child; in other words, to fabricate a snake-bite.

[*Macpherson, J.*—But surely snakes do not make such ugly holes.]

I do not for a moment suggest that the wound was made by a snake. But my theory is that it was made for the purpose of giving it the appearance of a snake-bite.

[*Macpherson, J.*—Every peasant in Bengal knows what a snake-bite is like. No one would mistake such a terrible wound for a snake-bite.]

My Lords, fortunately for my theory, I have got the very best evidence in support of it. Whether a genuine snake-bite would have such an appearance or not, it is needless for us to inquire, when tha fact is admitted that the prisoner himself attempted to pass it off as a snake-bite. He at any rate thought it might be taken for a snake-bite. And that is enough for my present purpose.

That the wound was inflicted after death is perfectly clear from the appearance of it and from the entire absence of blood; and that it was not made by any murderer is also clear from the superficial character of it. Why should any murderer inflict such a gentle wound with a spear, instead of thrusting it deeper? But if it was intended to fabricate a snake-bite, the superficial character of the wound is easily accounted for.

Mr. Ghose then read the Judge's charge and commented upon it, and concluded his address by remarking that if, by reason of the enormity of the crime alleged, and the absence of all cross-examination of the witnesses, the Court, after anxiously considering the evidence, could not see its way to acquitting the prisoner altogether, it might adopt another course, which the law allowed and which the Judge's summing up entitled the prisoner to ask for, viz., a new trial of the case before a fresh Jury.

No one appeared for the Crown in support of the conviction.

The learned Judges, after a few days' deliberation, delivered the following judgment :—

We are unable to confirm the conviction and sentence in this case, because the case was presented to the Jury by the learned Judge in a manner which seems to us open to grave objection.

The charge was one of murder by a father of his child; the only eye-witness of any part of the transaction was a child : there were many peculiarities about the case upon any view of it. The prisoner was undefended, and with the exception of one question to one witness, the witnesses were not cross-examined. In such a case the learned Judge would have done wisely to lay the case before the Jury with extreme caution, and to take great care that the Jury should not give undue weight to the evidence for the prosecution, or overlook or underrate its defects or incongruities. But the effect of the summing up of the learned Judge seems to us to have been to press unduly many points in the case against the prisoner, and to minimise the force of the objections to that case.

Almost at the beginning of the summing up the learned Judge deals with the question of motive for the alleged crime. He says—
"The adequacy of motive is no doubt a matter for your consideration,

but it is not a point which the prosecution is legally, or as a matter of law, bound to prove". This direction is perfectly correct. And if the learned Judge had stopped with that, his treatment of the subject of motive would have been open to no exception. But he in several parts of his summing up pressed upon the acceptance of the Jury a theory of motive which appears to us not supported by the evidence, and almost purely speculative.

In dealing with the question of probability, the learned Judge points out the improbability of the crime on the one hand, and of a false charge under the circumstances on the other. And he says—"Whichever hypothesis you adopt, a shock is given to ordinary experience and ordinary probability, and yet it is absolutely certain that one must be true". It is true that the learned Judge is careful to tell the Jury that they are to decide not on probabilities but on the evidence. But as far as probability is to weigh with these, it is left to them in the way we have pointed out. And the same mode of presenting the case is adopted in other parts of the summing up. Thus it is said—"If the child was not killed by the prisoner, the murder must have been committed by an outsider and an enemy". And the learned Judge goes on to point out the difficulties in the way of a conclusion that an outsider murdered the girl. Later on, speaking of the spear with which the Judge presumes the girl to have been murdered, he says—"Which theory best accords with ordinary experience and reasonable probability—the child's story that the murderer used his own spear, or the theory that an outsider used the prisoner's spear?" This is an extremely dangerous way of presenting a case to a Jury. When two alternative views are put before a Jury, one or other of which it is suggested must be true, the Jury are very likely to accept that alternative which seems more consistent with the probability and with the evidence. This is wrong for two reasons :—1st, Because it hardly ever happens that a Judge can safely assume that the alternatives he puts to the Jury necessarily exhaust the probabilities of the case ; 2ndly, Because it may be right that the Jury, by reason of the obscurity of the case, should refuse to adopt confidently any theory at all, and should on this ground acquit the prisoner.

In the early part of his summing up, the Judge says very correctly that the prosecution had to prove first "that the crime of murder was committed, and to establish in your minds a reasonable belief amounting to a moral certainty that the prisoner committed that crime". But in treating the case in detail, he throughout assumes that a murder was committed, and addresses himself to the question of "Who committed that?" This involves an assumption not only that the girl died from criminal violence, but that the circumstances were such that the crime amounted to murder. And this is an assumption which we think the Judge was not authorised in making.

Throughout the summing up, the circumstances adverse to the prisoner are pressed as strongly as possible, while those favourable to him seem to us not to have had due weight given to them.

The fact that no charge was made against the prisoner for several days after the occurrence is a very important fact. The learned Judge refers to it as the "single circumstance of importance that appears to throw doubt on the story as told by the prosecution". He then refers to the wife's explanation, but does not point out that that explanation is contradicted by the police officer. And he then goes on to offer several speculative explanations of her conduct which she herself never suggested. This great diversity in the mode of treating the facts on the one side, and those on the other, seems to us calculated seriously to prejudice the accused.

One material point of the evidence seems not to have been seriously considered at all. The learned Judge throughout his summing up assumes that death was caused by suffocation and a spear wound. The attention of the Jury was not called to the grave doubts arising on the evidence as to what was the real cause of death, and whether the spear-wound was inflicted before or after death, nor to the bearing of this question upon the whole case.

For these reasons we are unable to confirm the conviction and sentence. On the other hand, we do not think we should be justified in allowing the appeal and acquitting the prisoner. The safer course seems to us to be that the prisoner be tried again.

(Sd.)   A. WILSON.
(,,)   W. MACPHERSON.

13th June, 1882.

CHAPTER III

APPLICATION

FOR

THE TRANSFER OF THE CASE.

On the 7th July, 1882, Mr. Manomohan Ghose applied before Mr. Justice Maclean and Mr. Justice Macpherson, in the Calcutta High Court, for a rule calling upon Mr. Dickens, Sessions Judge of Nuddea, to show cause why the precept issued by him regarding the selection of certain Jurors named by him to sit on the trial of Muluk Chand Chaukidar should not be quashed, and why the case should not be transferred from the Court of Mr. Dickens to that of another Judge. The application was supported by the following affidavit :—

Affidavit of Baboo Prasanna Kumar Mittra.

1. That I am a pleader of the Judge's Court of Nuddea, and have obtained a *vakalutnama** from one Muluk Chand Sirdar Chaukidar, at present a prisoner awaiting his trial on a charge of murder, empowering me and other pleaders to defend the said prisoner.

2. That the said prisoner, Muluk Chand Chaukidar was, in May last, convicted by the Sessions Court of Nuddea of the offence of murder, and sentenced to death by the presiding Judge, P. Dickens, Esq.

3. That on the prisoner's appeal, and on the case being

---

* A power in writing authorising a pleader to appear on behalf of his client

referred by the Sessions Judge of Nuddea for confirmation of the sentence, a Division Bench of this Court, consisting of Mr. Justice Wilson and Mr. Justice Macpherson, set aside, on or about the 13th June, 1882, the sentence passed on the said prisoner, and directed his re-trial.

4. That within three or four days after the said order of re-trial reached Mr. Percival Dickens, Sessions Judge of Nuddea, I learnt from certain pleaders and other persons that Mr. Dickens had stated in open Court, within the hearing of my said informants, that he would select as Jurors Mr. Savi, Molla Khodadad, and others, who, in the Judge's opinion, were well qualified, to try the case of the said prisoner.

5. That at or about the same time, I also learnt that the Judge had stated to some of his ministerial officers, that, besides Mr. Savi and Molla Khodadad aforesaid, he would select Baboo Gopal Chunder Shaw, Mritunjoy Roy, and Baboo Haranath Mitter, to sit as Jurors to try the said case.

6. That on learning, as aforesaid, that the Sessions Judge intended to select Jurors according to his own idea of their qualifications to try the said case, and believing that such a proceeding would be illegal and might materially prejudice the prisoner, I felt it my duty to represent the matter to counsel in Calcutta, and, according to counsel's advice, Baboo Tarapada Banerjee, a pleader of the Judge's Court of Nuddea, and I, jointly presented, on the 20th June last, a petition to Mr. Dickens, Judge of Nuddea, an authenticated copy of which petition is annexed to this affidavit, and marked A :—

The humble petition of Muluk Chand Chaukidar, a prisoner in the Nuddea Jail—

Humbly sheweth,—That your petitioner has been informed that on receipt of the order of the High Court directing that your petitioner should be re-tried, your Honour stated in open Court that you would summon a special Jury for the trial of your petitioner, and that your Honour would summon for that purpose Mr. Savi, Molla Khodadad, and others.

Your petitioner begs respectfully to submit that there is no provision of law which authorises the summoning of a special Jury in the *mofussil* (country), nor is your Honour empowered by law to select any particular Juror or Jurors for the trial of any particular case at the Sessions.

Your petitioner therefore humbly prays that, on reconsidering the matter, your Honour will be pleased to direct that under the provisions of Section 407, Criminal Procedure Code, the Jurors to be summoned be chosen by lot in open Court out of the Jury list, and that at least fifteen or twenty persons may be so chosen for the purpose of being summoned to attend on the day of your petitioner's trial.

Your petitioner further prays that, considering the length of time he has been in *hajut* (prison), an early day may be fixed for his trial, and that, therefore, a special Sessions may be held for the purpose, if necessary, with the approval of the High Court.

And your petitioner, as in duty bound, shall ever pray.

7. That on the said 20th of June, I accompanied the said Baboo Tarapada Banerjee to the Judge's Court, when he presented the petition referred to in the preceding paragraph. He, Baboo Tarapada Banerjee, first stated to the Judge that he wished to apply for an early date being fixed for the trial of the prisoner, Muluk Chand Chaukidar, whereupon the Judge, Mr. Dickens, remarked that he could not conveniently try the case earlier than the 17th July. Baboo Tarapada Banerjee then said that his petition contained another prayer, namely, that the Jurors to be summoned might be selected by lot according to Section 407 of the Criminal Procedure Code. Mr. Dickens thereupon said—" I cannot have a number of pleaders to sit on the Jury," or words to this effect. Baboo Tarapada Banerjee then observed—" We do not want only pleaders to sit on the Jury, but we simply pray that the Jurors may be chosen by lot ". Mr. Dickens then said—" Why does not Mr. Ghose get the case transferred to Jessore or some other district ?" Baboo Tarapada Banerjee replied—" Jessore is not a Jury district. All that we want is that the Jurors should be chosen according to law." Mr. Dickens then said—" I have already formed my opinion

about the case. It would be difficult for me to change it, unless some strong evidence turns up in favour of the accused. It is very easy for a couple of Judges of the High Court, sitting with the record before them, to say what they like. . . . I have already held that two and two make four, and they cannot make me say that two and two make five," or words to this effect. He then asked— "What possible objection can there be to an English-knowing Jury? The Judge's charge loses half its force when translated into broken Bengalee. If the prisoner's chance of escape lies in an ignorant Jury, I am sorry for him," or words to this effect. Baboo Tarapada Banerjee observed—"The prisoner does not pray that an ignorant Jury should be selected. All that he asks for is that no special Jury-men be selected." Baboo Tarapada then read the first paragraph of the said petition which he held in his hand, and prayed for an order on the petition. Mr. Dickens, without questioning the correctness of the allegation contained in the first paragraph of the said petition, said—"The petition is in English; hand it over to me. I will consider the matter and pass orders afterwards." Baboo Tarapada Banerjee thereupon handed the petition to Mr. Dickens, who put it inside his box, saying—"If I am to be harassed by such petitions, and if my discretion as regards the selection of Jurors is to be fettered, I will write to the High Court to transfer the case from my file," or words to this effect.

8. On the next day, that is, the 21st June, 1882, Mr. Dickens passed an order on the back of the said petition, an authenticated copy of which order is also annexed to this affidavit, and marked B :—

"With reference to the matters urged in this petition, it is sufficient to say that the first Monday in the ensuing Sessions has been fixed for the commencement of the trial, and that the usual steps will be taken for securing the presence of a number of competent Jurors.

                                                     "P. DICKENS.

"*21st June, 1882.*"

9. I declare that, so far as I or Baboo Tarapada Banerjee have been able to ascertain, after careful and diligent inquiries in the Judge's office at Krishnaghur, Mr. Dickens has not chosen any Jurors by lot in open Court, for the purpose of their being summoned to attend on the date fixed for the trial of the said prisoner.

10. I have further ascertained that, on the 4th of July instant, the Judge issued a precept to the Magistrate of Nuddea, directing him to summon for the trial of the said prisoner the under-mentioned Jurors.:—

Mr. Savi, Molla Khodadad, Gopal Chunder Shaw, Umanath Ghosal, Mritunjoy Roy, Nakuleswar Bannerjee, Khirode Chunder Roy, Jodoo Nath Chatterjee, Bisweswar Chuckerbutty, Bipin Behari Mozoomdar, and Mati Lal Pal Chowdry.

11. That, to the best of my information and belief, the Jurors named above, or any of them, were not chosen by lot in open Court, and that in addition to four out of the five persons whom the Judge had originally selected, as stated in paragraphs 4 and 5 of this affidavit, he has chosen seven persons for the purpose of being summoned to attend on the 17th of July.

Paragraphs 12 and 13 are unimportant.

14. I further say that it is well known at Krishnaghur that Mr. Savi, one of the Jurors summoned, is a personal friend of Mr. Dickens, the Judge of Nuddea, and I verily believe that neither he nor Molla Khodadad, the two gentlemen named in the petition marked A, and now ordered to be summoned, will try the case fairly and impartially, and that neither of them ought to be selected as Jurors after what has transpired.

15. That I verily believe that, having regard to the strongly-expressed opinion of Mr. Dickens, the prisoner, Muluk Chand Chaukidar, will not have a fair and impartial trial before Mr. Dickens, the Judge, and that he will be materially prejudiced if the Jurors are selected according to the discretion of the Judge, instead of their being chosen by lot according to law.

16. I further say that I have shown this affidavit to the said Baboo Tarapada Banerjee, who has assured me that his recollection of what transpired on the 20th June, as described above, exactly tallies with what is stated in this affidavit.

Solemnly affirmed by me,

(Sd.) PRASANNA KUMAR MITTRA.

Mr. Ghose said that, having failed to avoid the necessity for bringing the matter before their Lordships, he now felt compelled to make this application, as that course was the only alternative left him. This matter had arisen out of the case tried by one of their Lordships, sitting in appeal with Mr. Justice Wilson, which resulted in the setting aside, on the 13th June last, of the sentence passed by Mr. Dickens upon the petitioner, and in an order for his re-trial.

In regard to the first of these prayers, the counsel explained that the Jury had been chosen, not by lot as prescribed by law, but selected by the Judge according to his own ideas of their competency. In the selection of Jurors, that officer maintained he had been guided by a desire that the fate of the accused should be placed in competent hands; but Mr. Ghose contended that, under Section 407 of the Criminal Procedure Code, in such a case, the Judge had no discretion. The Jury, under that section, should be summoned by lot, and in all his experience Mr. Ghose had found that Judges invariably followed that law strictly; indeed, this was the first time he had seen it disregarded. Nor could Mr. Dickens justify his departure from the law by urging, as he might, that this was not the first time he had so acted in regard to the formation of a Jury. The objection to this course, in addition to its being utterly illegal, was of a very serious character. It was not to be supposed that a Judge, in a case of this kind, would intentionally choose the Jurors from among persons who would sit to try the accused with a foregone conclusion of his guilt; but it was necessary that they should not be made to feel, by the compliment of a special selection, that they were qualified above others to sit upon the Jury. This implied compliment would have the effect, however imperceptibly, of warping their judgment, and influencing the verdict they would have to return. And this was a case in which that argument applied with more than ordinary force, from the fact that the Judge had expressed a very strong opinion against the prisoner, and sentenced him to death. The Judge's charge, on the last occasion, this Court had thought was open to grave objection; and if, in the new trial, the Jury were empanelled under a plan of favoured selection, such a course would be an avowed tribute to their intelligence, which would be sure to affect their judgment. But Mr. Ghose based his contention upon a higher ground. He submitted that Mr. Dickens' action was illegal, as being opposed to the terms of the section he had quoted; * and he would, therefore, ask their Lordships to set aside the precept issued by the the Judge. The prisoner had been placed in a difficult position, as no Juryman could be challenged without good and sufficient cause being shown to the Judge, whose decision upon the point was under the law final. Speaking from his own experience of criminal trials, Mr. Ghose could say that, generally, the Judges were anxious to have a body of Jurors to whom neither side objected. When, however, these are chosen by lot, the accused would, of course, have to take his chance.

Mr. Ghose submitted that it was difficult to conceive a stronger case for transfer than the present one. He said this with regret, as, originally, it was his own suggestion that the case should be returred

---

* S. 407 of Act X. of 1872 (the Criminal Procedure Code in force at the time) enacted :—" The Court of Session shall ordinarily, three days at the least before the time fixed for the holding of the Sessions, send a precept to a Magistrate directing him to summon as many persons named in the said revised list as seem to the Court to be needed for trials by Jury and trials with the aid of Assessors at the said Sessions, the number to be summoned not being less than double the number required for any case abou. to be tried at such Sessions.

" The names of the persons to be summoned shall be drawn by lot in open Court, excluding those on the revised list who have served within six months, unless the number cannot be made up without them ; the names so drawn shall be specified in the precept to the Magistrate."

to Nuddea for re-trial there. But at that time he had no idea how things would shape themselves, while Mr. Dickens himself was willing to be relieved from the task of trying the case a second time. Mr. Ghose was aware of the difficulties in the way of such a transfer, having regard to the prisoner's circumstances, and the fact that it would be harassing to the witnesses in the case if it were transferred to another district. He would, therefore, suggest to their Lordships a course which might be adopted to obviate these difficulties, viz., to request the Government of Bengal to depute some other Judge to Nuddea in order to try the case, which he expected would occupy not more than two days. This was the course adopted in the well-known Purneah case of *Abdul Kadir*, reported in XX. *Weekly Reporter*, p. 23, and was one to which the Crown could not object. As, the matter was urgent, and the trial was fixed for the 17th instant, he suggested that such explanations as their Lordships thought fit to call upon Mr. Dickens to make, might be made returnable as early as possible.

Mr. Justice Maclean.—But Prasanna Kumar Mittra does not pretend to have heard anything himself, beyond what occurred in his own presence on the 20th, when he presented the petition.

Mr. Ghose.—The truth of the rest is confirmed by the Judge's order on the petition presented to him on that day. That petition was drawn up in English, so that he should not have the excuse for saying he could not understand the vernacular. It set out that, as early as the 20th, we objected to two of the five Jurors nominated, and when that petition was read out to him, Mr. Dickens did not dispute or challenge the correctness of our statement that he had stated in open Court the names of the Jurors he intended to select.

Mr. Justice Maclean.—That may be accounted for by his refusing to answer in open Court an accusation against himself.

Mr. Ghose.—But if the petition contained so serious a charge, the learned Judge should have at once repudiated it, or done so in the order he passed subsequently. In it he draws a distinction between Jurors and "competent" Jurors.

Their Lordships granted Mr. Ghose's application, promising to issue the order in the course of the day, the terms of which, they said, would have to be carefully considered.

The rule came on for hearing on the 12th July, 1882, when no one appeared on behalf of the Crown or Mr. Dickens, to show cause. The learned Judges, after reading the written explanation submitted by Mr. Dickens, delivered the following judgment, transferring the case from Nuddea to Alipur in the suburbs of Calcutta:—

Maclean, J.—The prisoner's petition contains two prayers. The first is, that the precept for the summoning of the Jury for the trial of his case be quashed, on the ground that the Jurors named had not been chosen by lot out of the entire Jury list according to Section 407 of the Criminal Procedure Code. The second prayer is, " that inasmuch as it would be extremely inconvenient and harassing to your petitioner, and all the witnesses, if his case were transferred to another district, and inasmuch as by such transfer he would be deprived of the advantage of being defended by some of the local pleaders of Krishnaghur, who have kindly consented to defend him at the trial, this Court will be pleased to request the Government of Bengal to depute any Judge other than Mr. Dickens for the purpose of trying your petitioner's case in Nuddea on the 17th of July, or on any subsequent date ".

With reference to the first prayer, we have received a letter from the District Judge, in which he says that the precept was, as a matter of fact, issued under Section 410 of the Code, not 407 ; and he also justifies his procedure in summoning Jurors duly qualified on the ground that the practice has prevailed in his district for many years in critical cases without being questioned. He also points out that the prisoner in this case was tried on a previous occasion by a Jury summoned in precisely the same way in which it has now been objected to.

With reference to the precept having been issued under Section 410, that section provides for the summoning of Jurors at other periods than the period specified in Section 407, when the number of trials before the Court renders the attendance of more than one set of Jurors necessary. In this case, we understand that the ordinary Sessions of the Nuddea district commences on the 14th of this month. It therefore does not appear to us that there was any necessity for making use of Section 410; and if there had been, we are also of opinion that, although that section provides for the summoning of Jurors at times other than at Sessions, it does not say that the Jury is to be so summoned in any other than the method prescribed in Section 407.

As to the practice which is stated to have prevailed in the district of Nuddea for so many years, all we have to say is, that we recognise no practice except that which the law lays down. The law provides that, ordinarily, Jurors shall be drawn by lot in open Court; and although Section 408 provides for the summoning of special Jurors, that section only applies where the accused persons are entitled to be tried by a Jury constituted under Section 234—that is, a Jury *de medietate linguæ,* as it is called in other countries. If it were necessary, therefore, that the trial should proceed in the Nuddea Sessions Court, we should have thought it necessary to direct a fresh precept to be issued in the manner prescribed in Section 407. The prisoner has, however, requested to be tried at Nuddea by another Judge, but we think it inexpedient to apply to the local Government to depute any special Judge to try the case. The Judges of neighbouring districts have their own duties to perform, and we do not think that we could inconvenience the public service by asking that a special officer be deputed for the purpose of trying this case. We therefore propose to direct the trial of the case at the Alipur Sessions, which will commence on the 17th of this month; and we shall issue orders to the Judge of the district of Nuddea to transfer the case to the file of the Judge of Alipur, in order that the requisite steps may be taken to bring the case on during the ensuing Sessions. The Judge of Nuddea has stated that he has formed such an extremely decided opinion adverse to the prisoner, and has expressed it before the trial, that no trial before him, held on the same evidence, would be satisfactory either to himself or the accused. On these grounds we have less hesitation than we otherwise would have had in transferring the case.

Macpherson, J., who concurred generally with Maclean, J., said that Section 410 should be read along with Section 407, and there was nothing in the law to authorise the course which the Judge of Nuddea had taken. As Mr. Dickens favoured the transfer of the case, he concurred with Maclean, J., in transferring it to the Alipur Judge's Court.

Mr. Ghose asked their Lordships to direct the production of the police papers and the attendance of the medical witnesses from Nuddea, but was told to make his application to the Sessions Judge at Alipur, who would, their Lordships had no doubt, pass the necessary orders.

CHAPTER IV

RECORD OF THE SECOND TRIAL.

ALIPUR SESSIONS COURT.—21ST JULY, 1882.

(Before A. C. Brett, Esq., Additional Sessions Judge.)

THE EMPRESS *v.* MULUK CHAND CHAUKIDAR.

THE charge against the prisoner was that he, on the night of Monday, the 27th March, 1882, at Bhulat, in the Bongong sub-division, in Nuddea, intentionally caused the death of his daughter, Nekjan, aged about 9 years, by stabbing her with a spear, and thereby committed murder, an offence punishable under Section 302 of the Penal Code.

The prisoner pleaded " Not Guilty " to the charge.

The Government Pleader, Baboo Bipradas Banerjee, in opening the case, stated that the prisoner had once been convicted at Nuddea, but the High Court had thought fit to set aside the conviction and direct the re-trial of the prisoner in this Court. The case for the prosecution was that the prisoner had, on the afternoon of Monday, the 27th of March, sent away his wife from home for the purpose, it was said, of fetching some money from his brother, who lived in another village, and during his wife's absence from home, some time after midnight, killed one of his two daughters who were sleeping with him in the verandah of his house. It would be proved that the prisoner put his foot on the throat of the deceased child, Nekjan,

4

and then stabbed her with a spear. In the morning he called his neighbours and pretended that he did not know how the child had died, and set up snake-bite as the probable cause of death. He went to the *thanna* on the afternoon of Tuesday, and reported the death of his daughter as having been caused by snake-bite. The principal witness of the crime would be the prisoner's own daughter, who was sleeping with him that night, and who saw her father kill the deceased. This child told her mother the next morning, as soon as she returned home, and also told her aunt and another woman what she had seen, early on the Tuesday. These witnesses belonged, as it were, "to the enemy's camp," and they would come forward and prove these facts. It would also be proved that when the police arrived, on Wednesday morning, to investigate this matter, the prisoner took care to conceal his daughter, Golak, who had seen the murder committed, in an onion field, in order to prevent the police from examining her. The motive for the crime it would be difficult to prove, nor was it necessary to do so; but the Jury would be able to infer from certain facts, which would be proved, that the motive was probably to accuse one Kadam Ali Fakir, who had instituted criminal proceedings against the prisoner. The medical evidence showed that the wound in the abdomen was the cause of death, and if the Jury believed the evidence of the child they would convict the prisoner.

On the first witness being called, Mr. Manomohan Ghose, who appeared for the prisoner with Mr. Lalmohun Ghose, wished to know whether the prosecution intended calling Inspector Bipinbehari Chatterjee, who was the investigating officer, and who was then present in Court, as, in case of his being called as a witness, he ought to leave the Court.

The Government Pleader stated that he did not intend to examine the inspector.

The following witnesses were then examined :—

Witness No. 1.

Deposition of witness No. 1 for prosecution, DWARKA RAI, aged about 35 years, taken on solemn affirmation under the provisions of Act X. of 1873, before me, A. C. Brett, A.S.J. of the 24-Pergunnahs, this 21st day of July, 1882 :—

My name is Dwarka Rai. I am a constable. I know the prisoner. He is .Muluk Chand, *chaukidar* (watchman) of Bhulat. About 3 months ago I took the corpse of a little girl, said to be his daughter, and named Nekjan, from his house to Bongong, where I made it over to the native doctor, who made a *post-mortem* investigation of it in my presence. I brought these two weapons from prisoner's house [points to a spear and a *bagi* or large sacrificial knife] the day after I brought in the corpse. I found the spear stuck in the mat wall, and the *bagi* between the wall and the thatch.

Cross-examined by Mr. Ghose.—The prisoner came to the *thanna* (police station) where I was, about 3 or 4 in the afternoon of a day —I forget what day of the week, to report the death of his daughter. The *jemadar* (head-constable), Ramdas Sirkar, ordered me to go to the spot ; and I got to Bhulat after sunset that evening. Prisoner had preceded me. It was a stormy night, and I slept in the house of a barber named Modhu, not far from prisoner's house, and saw the body of a female child. On account of the storm I went to the barber's house. I saw no one but prisoner in his house, neither wife nor child, nor anyone ; I did not ask him where his family were. I did not see any relative of prisoner's about. I asked no questions about them, on account of the storm. When I came I had a light lit, and said—"I am going to stay and watch over the body," but when the storm came I could not remain, and went to the barber's. Once in the night, between 10 and 11, I went to see that the corpse was all right ; I found prisoner seated by it. A light was burning, but I did not take up the cloth to look at the corpse ; I went away. I told prisoner to be careful of jackals. He was alone. The storm had abated, but I went back to eat. Next morning, early, Ram Das, *jemadar* (head-constable), came. I remained with him during his investigation. He had the corpse out and examined it. Some neighbours were present, and some relatives of the prisoner, Jameer, Sajan, Sham Bahara, Uma Charan, were there. I forget whether Umesh Ghazee was there. I know Dhiru ; I do not know her husband, Umesh Ghazee, distinctly. I do not know him at all. [*Note by the Judge.*—For some reason or other the witness clearly fences with this matter.] I was not present when the head-constable had the prisoner's floor dug.

I had gone to call the *ryots* to carry the body. This was about 8·30 or 9 A.M. I was there about an hour. I forget the names of the men whom I brought to carry the corpse. Can't remember one. I don't know that the prisoner's floor was dug. This is the first time I hear of it. I can't say why, when I was asked if the head-constable had dug it, I said I was not there. [*Note by the Judge.*—Here again witness is evidently averse to tell the truth.] Even that day I did not see the prisoner's wife or child. [The witness is told that the day on which the body was sent in was Wednesday.] On Thursday morning the inspector told me that the case was one of murder, and he told me to go to Bhulat and investigate, and he would follow. The inspector said to me—"I hear from the doctor that death was caused by a spear ; you must search and see if you can find any such weapon". He also told me to bring prisoner's wife and daughter. I got to Bhulat at 9 A.M. I took the wife and the daughter, Golak, and started for Bongong. I met the inspector about two miles out of Bhulat. Besides prisoner's wife and daughter, I had with me Jameer, Sajan, Uma Charan, and Sham Bahara. I had been told by the inspector to bring respectable *ryots* (villagers), and therefore had these men with me. I started from Bhulat about 1 or 2 P.M. When I met the inspector I turned back with him. I cannot recollect whether I was present when the inspector recorded deposi-. tions. [*Note by the Judge.*—Witness fences again.] Before the arrival of the inspector I never asked prisoner's wife or daughter what they knew. When I left for Bhulat, on Thursday morning, I left prisoner at Bongong, also the men who carried the corpse. It was not Thursday that I met the inspector. It was on the Friday. On the Thursday night I remained with the prisoner's daughter, wife, and the others, at Bongong. What really happened was this : I met the inspector on the road with prisoner's wife and child with me, and he took them on to Bongong and sent me back for respectable *ryots*. No, this is really what happened : I met the inspector on the road on the Thursday, with the wife, child, &c., and we all went back to Bhulat. I forget where I stopped that night, or where the inspector stopped. I cannot say when the prisoner's wife and child got to Bongong. I forget whether I accompanied them to Bongong. I forget where they were on Friday. I forget where I was that day. The inspector came out to investigate on Thursday, but I cannot say what he did, as he sent me off for the *ryots*. I forget whom I brought. I forget what the inspector did after I brought the *ryots*. I can't say if they were brought. I can't say whether the inspector was in the village on Friday. I was present when the Magistrate investigated the case. There was only one spear exhibited in the case. No, there were two ; I only brought one.

Re-examined.—There is only one house in prisoner's premises. There are two verandahs. The corpse was in the north verandah. I have known the female witness, Dhiru, since the case. The inspector said to me—"The doctor says it is murder. You go and search for a spear, and if there is a wife of the prisoner, as you say there is, ask her what she knows about it ; also a child, and bring them to me." I forget where I saw prisoner again after I left him at Bongong. I forget how long after I was sent back to Bhulat the inspector came there. I cannot say whether it was that day or next day.

(Sd.)   A. C. BRETT.

Witness No. 2.

Deposition of witness No. 2 for prosecution, ADHAR CHANDRA CHAKRAVARTI, taken on solemn affirmation under the provisions of Act X. of 1873, before me, A. C. Brett, Esq., A.S.J. of the 24-Pergunnahs, this 21st day of July, 1882 :—

My name is Adhar Chandra Chakravarti. I am the native doctor of Bongong. On the 29th March last I examined the body of a female child, aged about 10, brought to me by Dwarka Rai, constable. The body was emaciated and liver enlarged. Decomposition had set in on the head only. The tongue slightly protruded, the teeth pressing the tongue lightly. The brain was congested slightly. I did not examine the condition of the throat. I made no detailed examination as to whether suffocation was the cause of death. I found a punctured incised wound over the epigastric region $\frac{1}{2}$ inch deep, and 1 inch by $\frac{1}{4}$ inch superficially. The wound appeared to have been inflicted by a weapon perpendicularly to the body. It had penetrated $\frac{3}{4}$ inch into the liver. The wound was exactly in the centre of the body. I saw the spear when I gave my evidence before the Magistrate. It then bore no trace, to my eye, of its having been lately sharpened. The spear I see before me might have caused the wound. The cause of death was this wound. I found blood extravasated in the peritoneal cavity of the abdomen, about three ounces. Both ventricles of the heart were empty. The body had some clothing on, but there was no blood on the clothing. There was no coagulated blood on the edges of the wound : no blood at all. The blood which I have said was in the peritoneal cavity was liquid, but I was unable to ascertain whether it was coagulated or not. I examined it carefully, but could find no coagulation. When the body was brought to me, a report was attached to it to the effect that death was supposed to have arisen from snake-bite. I found no trace of death by snake-poisoning. I told the police that the cause of death was the wound in the stomach, and gave it as my opinion that the child had been murdered. The constable, Dwarka, was present during the *post-mortem*, and I said to him at the time, "This is murder". I also wrote a report to this effect.

Cross-examined by Mr. Ghose.—I have been in medical service for eight years. My pay is Rs. 55 a month. I had to study medical jurisprudence. When the corpse came, the first thing I did was to look at the body. I felt sure that the wound in the belly, whatever produced it, was the cause of death. With that idea I made the *post-mortem*. I minutely examined the windpipe and lungs, but not the tissues of the throat. I formed no suspicion that suffocation or strangulation caused death. I saw no exterior marks on the throat. I made a minute examination of all the internal organs. There was no sign of any blood having flowed out of the wound. I have known cases in which, after an incised punctured wound inflicted during life, no blood has come out of the wound. Such wounds have caused death.

[*Note by the Judge.*—The witness gives instances, but they do not bear out his statement. One is of a case in which some wounds bled, but some did not ; and the other is a case in which the wounds bled only slightly.]

It is a main test in medical jurisprudence as to whether a wound has been inflicted during life or not, whether there is coagulation. But it is not *sine quâ non*. I should say the child had suffered from malarious fever. Enlargement of the liver produces pressure on the diaphragm, which may cause choking sensation, producing cough, but not suffocation. The wound was not triangular in shape. I see from looking at my report [reads] that I have entered in column 3 that the wound was triangular in shape, but that is an incorrect entry, and was inserted by me because the police reported it to be triangular. I filled up that report after I had finished the *post-mortem*. I never made any subsequent attempt to have the mistake rectified, or to tell anyone I had made it. I examined the body at 4 P.M. The girl might have been dead forty hours. *I did not think it necessary to examine the spinal cord. I did not do so.* It took me about two hours to make the *post-mortem.* Dwarka was present all along. The spleen was healthy. It was not congested. The kidneys were slightly congested. There was a mark as of a scratch on the left cheek. As soon as I saw the wound on the abdomen, and saw its shape and size, I felt sure it was not a case of snake-bite. I should say that from such a wound death might take place after from two to ten' hours. Death might be instantaneous. [After some deliberation says :] Instantaneous death might follow from a shock to the nervous system. I think it possible that the wound might have been inflicted immediately after death I am on friendly terms with inspector, Bepin Behari Chatterjee. I had no conversation with him about the case, either the day I examined the body or the day after. He did not ask me either on the 29th or 30th with what sort of a weapon the wound might have been inflicted.

Re-examined.—If blood had flowed from a wound, you could tell that it had done so 40 hours after.

Q.—Might not decomposition alter the shape of a wound?

A.—No.

Q.—Did you point out to the Magistrate that there was a mistake about the triangular wound?

A.—No, I did not think it was necessary.

By the Court.—When I saw the tongue protruding, I ascribed it to the effect of decomposition. The eyes also were congested. I also ascribed this to decomposition.

(Sd.)   A. C. BRETT.

Witness No. 3.

Deposition of witness No. 3 for prosecution, E. J. BRANDER, taken on oath before me, A. C. Brett, Esq., A.S.J. of the 24-Pergunnahs, this 21st day of July, 1882 :—

My name is E. J. Brander. I am civil surgeon of Nuddea. I have read the report of the native doctor in this case. I cannot say that his opinion is wrong. Congestion of the lungs—that of the brain, and that of the eyes,—protrusion of the tongue would be consistent with strangulation or suffocation, but would not necessarily lead to the inference of either. If a heavy man placed his foot on the neck of a little girl till she died, the above symptoms would probably be observed. Supposing a man acted in this way, and after pressing the girl's neck, for some time speared her, I should be surprised to find no hemorrhage externally. If the spear-wound were inflicted after partial suffocation had supervened, there would be more bleeding internally than externally, but there would have been some externally. I cannot conceive any wound causing a solution of continuity from the skin inwards taking place during lifetime, without producing some bleeding externally. On the hypothesis put before me, and if no artery had been cut, it is possible the external bleeding may have been slight.

Cross-examined by Mr. Ghose.—I received the report on the 1st April, two days after it was written. In that report it is not mentioned that there were no marks of external bleeding. After reading all the details of the native doctor's report, I do not think the materials are sufficient for us to predicate that the wound was inflicted during life or after death. A wound in the abdomen might be made to gape by the pressure of the gases generated during decomposition. After forty hours, in March, I should expect to find such gases. Coagulation is a main test as to whether a wound was inflicted during life, but decomposition tends to liquify coagulated blood. Excluding the shape of the wound, there is nothing in the symptoms detailed in the report inconsistent with death from snake-bite. Protrusion of the tongue and eyes would be produced by decomposition. It would be very difficult, twenty-four hours after death, to say whether the eyes were congested or not.

Q.—Supposing the child had been bitten by a snake on the abdomen, had died, and that some one very soon after death had enlarged the wound, is there anything in the symptoms inconsistent with this?

A.—No.

Re-examination.—No questions.

By Court.—I said before the Sessions Judge of Nuddea—"The ventricles of the heart are reported empty. Bleeding, therefore, must have supervened. It may have been internal." By this I did not mean to exclude the question of external bleeding to a visible extent. I was not asked about external bleeding, and my mind was directed to the fact that the dangerous bleeding would probably be internal.

I do not think the native doctor was justified in saying that the case was not one of snake-bite, because he did not notice that the body had turned black, or that the nails were shrivelled.

(Sd.) A. C. BRETT.

The Court here adjourned till the next day.

SECOND DAY'S PROCEEDINGS.

Witness No. 4.

The deposition of witness No. 4 for prosecution, GOLAK MANI, aged about 6-7 years, taken before me, A. C. Brett, Esq., A.S,J. of 24-Pergunnahs, this 22nd day of July, 1882.

[*Note by the Judge.*—The child says to tell a lie is a "*pâp*" (sin). She does not know what a "*pâp*" means; but she is intelligent.] My name is Golak Mani. I know the prisoner. He is my father. His name is Muluk Chand. I had a sister named Nekjan, a little older than myself. My mother left home in the afternoon, taking a younger sister and an infant brother of mine. My father, Nekjan, and I went to sleep on a mat in the verandah facing the cow-path. In the night I was awakened by my sister kicking me. She was kicking her feet about when I awoke, and my father had his foot on her throat, and then stuck a spear into her. I said to him—"Why are you beating her?" He said—"Lay the blame on the Fakir Kadam Ali". My father had an intrigue with this man's wife, Sarba. My sister kicked her legs about, but could not speak. It was a moonlight night. The moon was setting. It was near dawn. My sister could not move, and I concluded she was dead. After this my father went out. I remained with my sister's body. About dawn my *nâni* Haru Bebee, the mother of Amrita, came. I told her my father had killed my sister. Dhiru called me to go and eat, and I went to her. She called to me from near a date-tree in the cow-path. I told her what my father had done. When the day was well on, my mother came home. I told her what my father had done. I was at Sham Mehtar's house when my mother returned. I had gone to bathe. I mean I was at home when my mother returned.

Q.—Do you know when the police came?

A.—I was in the onion field. I am in the habit of looking after the onions, and I went there of my own accord. I did not see my sister's body taken away.

Q.—When did you return from the onion field?

A.—About noon, after the corpse had been taken away.

Cross-examined by Mr. Ghose.—The *barra · darogah* (chief inspector of police) taught me the word "*páp*". He said—"*Mitya bolile páp hai ; satya bola bhala*".* He told me this at Bongong. He said to me—"*Páp hoile ki hoy?*"† At Nuddea I was told by my mother that my father had been sentenced to be hanged. On that day my mother made an offering at the foot of a sacred tree near the court, and gave me some of the sweetmeats which she offered. I have remained with my mother ever since the case. We have not been to visit my father in the jail. When I opened my eyes and saw my father killing my sister, I did not sit up. I watched him keeping lying down. [*Note by the Judge.*—The child is made to show the exact position she kept, and lies down with one hand very slightly raising her head.] I talked to my father in this position. I was still in this position when my father went out. I did not go to sleep, but remained lying down. I did not get up to pass water either before or after the deed. I did not want to. I remember giving evidence before the Magistrate at Bongong. I there said that I had awoke because I wished to pass water, but it was a mistake of memory (*mone cheela na* ‡). I did tell the Magistrate that I was awoke by my sister kicking me. I saw my father take the spear from the roof. It was kept in a place where you could reach to it with the hand from the bed. The mother of my mother is alive. She is called Koti in the village ; and her house is on the other side of the road from ours. [*Note by the Judge.*—The child evinces a curious reluctance to answer whether her mother's mother is alive, and says at first that she must ask her mother.] I did not call her when I saw my sister killed. I did not cry out at all when I saw my sister killed. I wept a little. I did not tell my grandmother, Koti, what I had seen. I never told her. Haru Bebee is my *darham náni* (called grandmother, but not related). I never told anyone in my village what I had seen except Haru, Dhiru, and my mother. I have

---

* " Sin is incurred if one tells a lie." † " What happens if sin is incurred ?"

‡ " Did not remember."

playmates in the village. I never told them anything of what had happened. After my father returned, having gone out after the deed, he found me seated by my sister on the bed, awake. He did not call out to me—"Golak! get up". He began to cry. He called out loudly—"Oh, my neighbours, how is it my Nekjan is dead!" Dhiru is the wife of Umesh-Ghazee, and is sister of my mother. The first person to come, on my father's calling out, was Haru Bibi.

Q.—What men came?

A.—Jameer, Sajan, and Sham Mehtar. They are not related to us. My uncle, Umesh Ghazee, came, looked at the corpse, and went away. [*Note by the Judge.*—The child seems very reluctant to say that this man came.] Umesh and my *nani*, Koti, live in the same premises. I did not tell him what had happened. I did not tell anyone that my father had told me to lay the blame on the Fakir. My mother has never asked me why my father killed Nekjan. [Ram Dass, head-constable, is called in.] This *darogah* ordered the floor of our house to be dug up, and my uncle, Umesh Ghazee, dug it up with a *kodali* (spade). My mother was there. I was there. The floor was dug in order to look for the snake which was supposed to have bitten my sister. Everyone supposed this. I did not say anything of what I had seen. The *darogah* did not ask my mother how Nekjan had died. [Dwarka Rai, constable, is called in.] This constable took me and my mother into Bongong. We got there at night. I saw the inspector there. [Identifies Inspector Bipin Behari, who is called in.] I was taken to him yesterday evening after I had been in attendance at this Court. I and my mother were taken. The inspector told me to tell him what I knew, and I related to him what I have said here. I don't know what my mother said to him. We were taken in one by one. Yesterday week my mother and I were seated under a tree near Bongong, and Kadam Ali Fakir was with us, giving us water. Kadam Ali has come in with us here. He is outside the court.

Re-examined.—I call Koti my *nani*. She was at home when my sister was killed. She did not come. Her foot was swollen. [*Note by the Judge.*—This explanation is given with much hesitation, and after several unintelligible sentences on the part of the child.] The corpse was in the yard (*utan*) when the floor was dug up.

(Sd.) A. C. Brett.

Witness No. 5.

Deposition of witness No. 5 for prosecution, BARAHTI, aged about 33 years, taken on solemn affirmation under the provisions of Act X. of 1873, before me, A.'C. Brett, Esq., A.S.J. of the 24-Pergunnahs, this 22nd day of July, 1882 :—

My name is Barahti. I am the wife of the prisoner at the bar. I had a daughter Nekjan. , She was aged about 8 or 10. I went to Goga to get money, by direction of my husband, on account of a case he had with Kadam Ali Fakir. He told me to go to his brother. His brother said he had none. I went in the afternoon, and returned home next morning about 8 or 9. When I came to my house, I found my daughter, Golak, seated on a mat in the verandah, silently weeping, and by her, on the same mat, was the corpse of my daughter, Nekjan. My husband was not there. The corpse was covered with the child's clothes, but these were not worn ; the body was naked. I saw no blood, but I saw a wound in the abdomen. [Indicates on her own person the locality.] My husband came in some time after. When I came and saw my child dead and the other child by the body, I said to Golak—" How is it your sister is dead ? " She said her father had killed her sister. She said he had placed his foot on her throat and then speared her. When my husband came in I said to him—" I left my children with you. You sent me off to Goga for money ; now tell me who killed my child." I further said to him—" I have no quarrel with anyone ; you have a quarrel with the Fakeers ". He said—"I don't know who killed her ; I was not at home ". He further said—" What has been done has been done ; now let us try to save ourselves ". This spear and this *bagi* (sword) now before me are my husband's.

Cross-examined by Mr. Ghose.—My husband was fond of Nekjan. I did not find my husband crying when I returned. I did not see him cry at all. I did not say to the Judge at Nuddea—" I heard cries ; my child Golak was crying, and my husband was also crying". He never cried [emphatically]. I did not tell the Judge of Nuddea that " I first had a conversation with my husband, and that I then asked Golak how her sister had been killed ". What I say now is true. I spoke to Golak first. When I saw my husband, I said to him—" Golak says you killed Nekjan ". He denied it. I did not ask Golak why her father had killed Nekjan. She did not tell me. I saw my mother, Koti, about noon that day, and I said to her—" I left two children alive, and find one dead ". She said—" Well, you will not get the child alive again ; probably the author of its being has killed it ". When I came home I saw the child dead, and I had no idea before I saw the corpse that anything had happened. I found Golak alone by the body. No villager, neighbour, or relation was there. I did not tell anyone in the village what Golak had told me. I told my mother only. Ram Dass, head-constable, came to our house the next day. He asked me nothing. I told him nothing. This is he. [Identifies Ram Dass, who is called in.] My husband told me to go in when this constable came. [*Note by the Judge*—This she says of her own accord.] I went into another hut of ours. Umesh Ghazee dug the floor of our verandah by order of Ram Dass. I saw from some distance. I heard my husband tell the police that Nekjan had probably died from snake-bite. It was on a Tuesday I returned. On the next Thursday was the first time I told the police my husband had killed Nekjan. I did so to Dwarka, constable, in my house, in the presence of the *punchayet*, Uma Charan. Dwarka took me and Golak to Bongong. He accompanied us on the road. He also took Jameer, Sajan, and Uma Charan. Dwarka asked me in my village how my daughter had died, and I then told him her father had killed her. We got to Bongong in the evening. Dwarka was with us. He took us to the inspector (*burra darogah*) at his house. I had never seen the inspector before. Dwarka kept us at the *thanna* (police station) that night. Next morning (Friday) my statement was recorded, and Golak's statement was recorded.

Q.—As you were being taken off, after your statement was recorded, did you see your husband in custody ? and did you call out to him—" Is it true that you have confessed to the police that you killed your daughter?"

A.—Yes ; I said so. [*Note by the Judge.*—The witness afterwards retracts this, but in a very unsatisfactory manner.] I did not say any such thing to my husband, nor did I hear from him that this was false. The police did not tell me that my husband had made a confession. After my husband was sentenced to death, I did not go to see him. Some one about the court asked me if I would appeal. I was told that an appeal would not save my husband's life. I therefore took no steps to appeal. The people in the Court told me that an appeal would cost nothing. I made no offering to a saint after my husband was convicted. I was not taken to the inspector's house last night.

My daughter, Golak, was not taken. She remained with me. If my daughter has said that she and I were taken yesterday, one by one, to the inspector, it is because she is a child. If she has said that I made an offering, I cannot explain it. Last Friday week I did not sit under a tree with 'Kadam Ali Fakir. He is now staying in the same house with me at Alipore.

Re-examined.—I cannot say why he has come in. His wife has come in.

By Court.—I was very angry with my husband when I found he had killed my child. I said I would never give him food again, and he said he would never take food from me again. When I saw the police come, and saw that my husband was trying to make them believe that my child had died of snake-bite, I did not come forward and tell the true story, because I was not called (*"Amár dák hoe nai"*). The wound on the body was long, not triangular. It was wide enough open to admit a finger. I told the Magistrate at Bongong that I suspected my husband had killed Nekjan, in order to bring a charge against Kadam Ali Fakir. My daughter Golak had told me that when she asked her father why he struck Nekjan, he had said—"The blame will be round the neck of Kadam Ali". I told this both to the Magistrate and to the Judge of Nuddea.

[*Note by the Judge.*—No indication of any such statement is to be found either in the record of the committing officer or in that of the Judge of Nuddea.]

(Sd.)   A. C. Brett.

Witness No. 6.

Deposition of witness No. 6 for prosecution, HARU, aged about 40 years, taken on solemn affirmation under the provisions of Act X. of 1873, before me, A. C. Brett, Esq., A.S.J. of the 24-Pergunnahs, this 22nd day of July, 1882 :—

My name is Haru Bibi. I am the widow of Fatik Sardar. I remember when Nekjan died. I know the prisoner. He is Muluk Chand. His house is so far from mine. [Indicates, say, 150 yards.] I heard the voice of a child from prisoner's house, early in the morning, saying—"Who has killed my sister?" She was crying and saying this. She did not raise her voice higher than this. [Indicates a decidedly low pitch.] She was not crying so as to attract help. I was in my own house. I went to prisoner's house. I found the corpse of Nekjan lying on a mat in the verandah, and her sister, Golak, was sitting by it crying. Golak said to me—"My father has killed Nekjan by thrusting a spear into her, and has thrown the spear into the kachu jungle". She also said he had placed his foot on Nekjan's neck. The prisoner was then seated close to Golak, and when she said this, he got up and lifted his hand at her in a threatening manner, but did not strike her. I saw no wound on the corpse. I did not tell the Judge of Nuddea or the Magistrate of Bongong that I had seen a wound.

Cross-examined by Mr. Ghose.—There is no man in my house. I am not on friendly terms with prisoner or his family. They have not set up any *dharm* relationship with me. I did not tell any-one what the child had said to me. When prisoner threatened to strike Golak, he did not say anything. He did not say—"I will put my foot on your throat". [*Note by the Judge.*—That appears from the Judge's record.]

Prisoner was crying.

Re-examined.—I became a widow before Nekjan died.

(Sd.) A. C. BRETT.

Witness No. 7.

The deposition of witness No. 7 for prosecution, DHIRU, aged about 40 years, taken on solemn affirmation under the provisions of Act X. of 1873, before me, A. C. Brett, Esq., A.S.J. of the 24-Per-gunnahs, this 22nd day of July, 1882 :—

My name is Dhiru Bibi. My home is at Mouzah Bhulat. I am the wife of Umesh Ghazee. Barati is my full sister. The prisoner at the bar is her husband. My house is about so far from theirs. [Indicates, say, 300 yards.] About 8 in the morning I called Golak to come to me to eat ; she was crying, and told me that her father had killed Nekjan. Before that I had heard her cry, and had looked out, and had seen Nekjan's corpse lying in the verandah. Seeing this I turned back. Golak told me that her father had put his foot on Nekjan's throat. She said nothing about a spear.

Cross-examined by Mr. Ghose.—I do not know whether my husband went to prisoner's house on hearing cries. My husband slept with me that night. My house is in the same premises as prisoner's. It is true—I remember now that my husband went to prisoner's house before I did. He returned, and then I went. I did not tell anyone what I had heard from Golak. I did not tell my husband. My husband slept with me the following night. The common talk in the village was that Nekjan had died from some unknown cause. The day after the event my husband took a *kodali* (spade) to prisoner's house to dig up the floor. I don't know why. I did hear from my husband that it was to look for the snake that was supposed to have killed Nekjan. I did not then tell him what Golak had told me. I did hear prisoner crying before I went. [*Note by the Judge.*—Here the witness very suddenly faints, and is taken out; no one wishes to ask her any further questions.]

(Sd.)   A. C. BRETT.

The Court here adjourned till Monday, the 24th July.

THIRD DAY'S PROCEEDINGS.

Witness No. 8.

The deposition of witness No. 8 for prosecution, SARBA, aged about 28 years, taken on solemn affirmation under the provisions of Act X. of 1873, before me, A. C. Brett, Esq., A.S.J. of the 24-Pergunnahs, this 24th day of July :—

My name is Sarba. My home is at Mouzah Bhulat. I know the prisoner. He is Muluk Chand. He came to me one night when my husband was away, and I was asleep by myself. He put his hand indecently on my body, and I called out. My mother-in-law came and caught him by the cloth, and he snatched away his clothing from her and ran away. My mother-in law lit a lamp, and we saw a spear in the verandah where I was sleeping. It was not my husband's, and we inferred that prisoner had left it. My husband laid a complaint against prisoner on account of this.

Cross-examined by Mr. Ghose.—I forget how long before I heard of Nekjan's death this occurred. It was less than a month. I did not tell the Magistrate that my mother-in-law had snatched the spear from prisoner. I forget if I said so. I have a female cousin named Otiran, who is wife of Meeru. Prisoner and Meeru have had a case, which prisoner won. After prisoner had won this case, my husband accused him of trespass into our house with intent to outrage my modesty.

Re-examined.—No questions.

(Sd.)   A. C. BRETT.

Witness No. 9.

The deposition of witness No. 9 for prosecution, UMA CHARAN SIRCAR, aged about 40 years, taken on solemn affirmation under the provisions of Act X. of 1873, before me, A. C. Brett, Esq., A.S.J. of the 24-Pergunnahs, this 24th day of July, 1882 :—

My name is Uma Charan Sircar. My father's name is Bangsidhar. My home is at Mouzah Bhulat, where I am a cultivator.

I am a village *punchayet*. I know the prisoner. He is Muluk Chand, *chaukidar* of our village. On the morning of a day about the 15th Chait last, Umesh Gazee came to me and said—"Nekjan, the daughter of Muluk Chand, is lying dead; you are requested to come by Jameer, Sajan, Sham Mehtar, and Muluk Chand himself". I went. I saw the child lying dead in the verandah. A cloth was over her. I asked prisoner how she had died, and he said he could not say. I made him remove the cloth, and I saw a wound on it here. [Points to slightly above the abdomen.]

Question by Court.—Was this the shape of the wound [triangular mark]?

A.—It was [triangular].

I asked the prisoner how this wound had been caused, and he said he could not tell. After a little time he said the child had died from snake-bite. He did not say that the wound was the mark of the bite. He showed me holes in his house, and said the snake might have come out of one. As I came up to the house I saw a spear in some kachu * jungle by the cow-path. I saw a *bagi* some distance off. It was behind the house of Sharup Ghosh. I told the prisoner these weapons were to be left as I saw them, and I told him to go to the police and report. I asked him why these weapons were lying there. He said he could not tell. When I told him to go to the police to report, I also told him to go to my house and get an *ittila* (notice) from me, which I said I was going home to write; but he did not come to me.

Cross-examined by Mr. Ghose.—Ram Das, head-constable,

* Arum Colocasia.

5

came the next day, and I was taken to him by Dwarka Rai at prisoner's house last of all the witnesses. The corpse had then been placed on a litter. I did not tell Ram Das that I had seen the weapons. I felt some suspicion when I saw the weapons. I suspected that some one had killed Nekjan. I cannot say whether I told the Judge of Nuddea that I suspected the prisoner. It is a long time ago. If I had thought there would be so much fuss, I would have taken a note of what I said. [*Note by the Judge.*—This remark is made by witness of his own accord when pressed by the counsel. He fences very much with the questions relating to whether he suspected the prisoner.] When I went to Ram Das, head-constable, I did not notice whether the spear and *bagi* were where I had seen them. In fact, prisoner had said to me, when I said they were to remain in *statu quo*—" They are my things; I will take them away when I like ". I forget whether I ever said this before in any Court. I have been lately made a *punchayet*, and I did not know that it was my duty to report murders ; this is why I did not tell Ram Das what I knew. I was taken by Dwarka Rai to Ram Das, but I had absolutely no conversation with him. I did not ask him why I had been sent for. [*Note by the Judge.*—After a prolonged silence, whilst the Court is recording witness' previous statement, he says of his own accord :] Afterwards, a little afterwards, Ram Das asked me if I knew how the child had died. I said I did not know. I did not tell him I had any suspicion. When I first went and saw the corpse I asked prisoner where deceased and her sister Golak had slept. Golak was not there. I don't know how I knew that Golak and Nekjan had slept together. I did not see the floor dug up when I was taken to Ram Das. I did not go near enough to see. I saw no blood on the body or clothes. Goga village is a *koss* off (2 miles) from our village. I hear prisoner's brother lives there.

No re-examination.

By Court.—I saw the spear and *bagi* after leaving prisoner's house. The spear was north of his house, and the *bagi* was 3 *rashis* (120 yards) west. My house is south of his. When I asked the prisoner how the wound had come, I then had my suspicion aroused, but I had not seen the weapons then. I suspected because I saw a wound. When I got home I did not commence to write an *ittila* (notice). As prisoner did not come, I wrote none. If I had written one, I should have said in it—" I have seen the corpse of

Nekjan ; her father says she died by snake-bite : but as I see a wound, I suspect murder ". I should not have said that I suspected anyone in particular.

(Ṣd.)   A. C. BRETT.

⸰ Witness No. 10.   ⸰

The deposition of witness No. 10 for prosecution, RAM DAS SIRKAR, taken on solemn affirmation under the provisions of Act X. of 1873, before me, A. C. Brett, Esq., A.S.J. of the 24-Pergannahs, this 24th day of July, 1882 :—

My name is Ram Das Sirkar. I am a head-constable. On the 27th March I was posted at Sarsa Thanna, which is 9 or 10 ten miles from Bhulat. On the 28th March, about 3 P.M., the prisoner Muluk Chand came to me and laid an information. This is it. [Identifies and reads a paper, now marked X.] It was written under my supervision and signed by me. I was then taking charge from the sub-inspector, and I sent Dwarka Rai, constable, with the prisoner to Bhulat ; Dwarka and prisoner went off together. I followed next morning about 7 or 7·30. I found the body of a little girl lying in prisoner's north verandah. She was said to have been named Nek-jan. The tongue was protruding, the eyes half closed, and there was a triangular wound on the abdomen so big [triangular mark]. [Witness draws a triangle of this size.] I sent the corpse in by Dwarka Rai, constable. I remained at Bhulat to take my meals, and I left at 4 P.M. No blood was on the body or the clothes.

Cross-examined by Mr. Ghose.—When I arrived at Bhulat a number of respectable persons were assembled by the body. This man [identifies last witness] was present. He is Uma Charan, punchayet. I made prisoner stretch the triangular wound, and I then carefully looked into it, and saw that it had no depth. It looked only skin-deep. I asked the by-standers what they thought was the cause of death, and they all said that they thought it must be snake-bite. I asked Uma Charan, and he said the same. Prisoner's wife was there. I asked what she knew. She said—" I was not there. I cannot say how the child died." I held a sura-thal (inquest) about 9·30, and then sent the body in.

By Court.—This is the report I wrote of the sura-thal. [Identifies and reads a paper marked G by the Judge of Nuddea.] There was froth at the mouth, and the stomach was distended.

The body was not stinking. The names of Uma Charan and Nek-jan's mother are appended to exhibit C. If Nekjan's mother, Barati, has said that she did not see me or speak to me at that time, she has told a lie. I was prepared to accept the fact that the child had died from snake-bite, but I was not quite sure. The villagers and I thought that the wound might be a snake-bite. By my order a man, who I have been told is Umesh Ghazee, dug up the floor. [Refers to the police diary containing an entry to that effect.] He came across some holes, apparently snake-holes, and followed them up without finding any snake. As far as I remember, Dwarka Rai was present when the digging took place. The digging was commenced after Dwarka Rai had brought in the men I wanted. No one told me anything about a *bagi* or a spear. I saw no reason to suspect the prisoner. On the morning of the 31st March, a *chaukidar* brought me an order from the inspector to prepare a "first information," accusing prisoner of having killed his daughter, and the inspector stated in the order that he was himself about to investigate. I was at Sarsa when I got this order. I went to Bhulat, expecting to meet the inspector there, but not finding him, I went on to Bongong. When I got to Bhulat, I heard that the prisoner's wife and child had been taken in by a constable to Bongong. I did not hear that the inspector had been at Bhulat. On thinking, I remember that in the *purwana* (order in writing) there was no mention of prisoner having killed his child; only that the doctor reported the case to be murder. I found Dwarka Rai at Bongong when I got there. He told me that prisoner's daughter said the prisoner had killed Nekjan. He told me that the child had said this when she was brought before the inspector at Bongong. On the 31st I went with the inspector to Bhulat. As far as I know, this was the first time the inspector went to Bhulat. When I first went to see the body, the prisoner told me that he had slept that night with his two children, Nekjan and Golak. This was in the presence of the villagers. As Golak was a child, I made no inquiries about her. It was the case for the prosecution at Bongong and Nuddea that Golak had been concealed by prisoner in the onion field to prevent my questioning her. I do not remember whether the inspector received any order from the district superintendent to ask me for an explanation as to why I had not examined Golak. I don't know whether the inspector reported that the reason was because prisoner had concealed the child in an onion field. I don't remember whether the inspector questioned me on the matter. I told the Magistrate I did not find Nekjan's sister—I meant to say that I did not look for her.

No re-examination.

By Court.—I heard that the doctor said the wound was deep. I did not tell the Magistrate or the Judge that I had examined it, and found it not deep. I heard that the doctor said the wound must have been caused by a sharp instrument. I did not hear that he said a spear might have caused it. I saw this spear in the Court. It did not strike me that this was the weapon said to have been used. I did hear that the case for the prosecution was that the child had been killed with a spear. I did not think how strange it was that a spear could produce a triangular wound. When I told the Judge of Nuddea that the edges of the wound were open, I meant that the skin did not meet, but was open.

(Sd.)   A. C. Brett.

Ex. X. First Information.

28th March, 1882, 3 P.M.—Muluk Chand, *chaukidar*, aged 40 or 41 years, of Bhulat, arrived at the station and deposed as follows :—Yesterday my wife was not at home. I was sleeping last night with my daughter Nekjan, aged 8 or 9 years, in the east verandah of my house. At one *prahar* of the night remaining (3 A.M.), I went to look after my onion field, which is about 20 *rashis* (800 yards) to the north of my house, leaving the said daughter asleep in the verandah. At dawn when I returned home, I found my daughter lying dead in bed, froth coming out of her mouth. On examining her condition, I found on her stomach a slight mark as of a cut or bite ; her colour had turned blue ; no other mark or wound was apparent on the body. I am not aware of the cause of death ; and I have no suspicion regarding her death. This is my statement. I do not know to read or write.

+ Muluk Chand,
Chaukidar of Bhulat.

Ex. C.,

Inquest Report on the Death of Nekjan Chokri.

29th March, 1882, 7 A.M.—In the presence of Prahlad Ghosh, Sajan Mandal of Bhulat, Jameer Mandal, Atar Ghazee, Amiruddi

Ghazee, Kalu Ghazee, and Uma Charan Sircar, *punchayet*, and other *ryots* of the village, and Barati, mother of deceased, and Muluk Chand, the father, I saw the corpse lying in the north verandah of the east facing house, covered with a piece of cloth. I caused the corpse to be brought down to the yard, and after uncovering it I observed as follows :—Age about 8 or 9 years, dark complexion, long hair on her head, stomach swollen, the tip of the tongue between the teeth, froth issuing from the mouth and nostrils, emaciated in appearance, a triangular mark of a cut or bite below the chest, measuring the breadth of one finger ; eyes shut. No other mark or wound on the body.

(Sd.)   RAM DAS SIRCAR,

Head-Constable, Sarsa Police Station.

EXAMINATION OF THE ACCUSED PERSON.

The examination of MULUK CHAND CHAUKIDAR, aged about 35 years, taken before me, Gopal Chandra Mukerji, Deputy-Magistrate, 1st class, at Bongong, on the 31st day of March, 1882 :—

My name is Muluk Chand Chaukidar. My father's name is Ashruf Sirdar. I am by caste Mahomedan, and by occupation *chaukidar.* My home is at Mouza Bhulat.

Q.—Did you murder your daughter Nekjan?

A.—No ; I did not kill her.

Q.—On what date, and when did she die ?

A.—Early on Tuesday I went to look after my onion field ; no one was in the house except the two girls ; my wife had gone to Goga on Monday afternoon. On my return from the field I saw my eldest daughter, Nekjan, lying at a little distance from her bed. I called her, but she did not answer. I felt her body, but she did not move. When it was daylight, I saw that she had a wound, and was dead, and my daughter, Golak Jan, was asleep. I began to cry. At four or six *dandas* of the day (8 A.M.), I was going to the *thanna* when I was arrested by a *piada* (peon) on the complaint of Kadam Ali Fakir, who had taken out a warrant against me.

Q.—After that, when did you go to the *thanna* ?

A.—After midday I went to the *thanna* and informed the *daroga* (police inspector).

Q.—How far is the *thanna* from your house ?

A.—Four or four and a half *kos* (8 or 9 miles).

Q.—When did you leave your daughters and go to the field?

A.—When there was one *prahar* of the night remaining (3 A.M.).

Q.—Why did you send your wife away from your house?

A.—To obtain money, with a view to defray the expenses of the case that was pending against me.

Q.—Is this spear yours?

A.—Yes.

Q.—Why does it look as if it had been rubbed?

A.—I cannot say; I did not rub it. I did not take it with me to the field. I took my *latti* (stick).

Q.—When you go to the field or to your watch, do you carry the spear or the *latti?*

A.—Sometimes I take the spear, sometimes I take the *latti* (stick).

Q.—Whom do you suspect having killed your daughter?

A.—I did not see anyone killing her, and my suspicion does not fall on anyone; but I have a quarrel with Kadam Ali Fakir and Mirun.

Q.—How many spears have you got?

A.—Only this one; the other one has been falsely produced as mine.

Q.—Had your daughter any ornaments on her person?

A.—No.

EXAMINATION OF THE ACCUSED AT THE PREVIOUS TRIAL.

Under Section 34? of the Criminal Procedure Code, by Mr. Dickens, Sessions Judge of Nuddea, dated the 16th May, 1882:—

My name is Muluk Chand Chaukidar. My father's name Ashruf Chaukidar; by caste Mussulman; inhabitant of Goga, Thanna Sharsha, at present residing at Bhulat.

Q.—Are you guilty of the charge?

A.—I am not guilty.'

Q.—Did you make this statement before the Deputy-Magistrate, and is it correct? [Read exhibit D.]

A.—Yes, I made this statement, and it is correct.

Q.—Why did you send your wife to Goga, instead of going there yourself?'

A.—Lest the police should find me absent from the village, and beat me; through fear of this I did not go.

Q.—Why did you not go during the day?

A.—They (my people at Goga) do not stay at home during the day, but go out to the field, &c., and cannot be found at home during the day, so I did not go during the day.

Q.—You have said that you saw, on your return from the field at night, that your daughter was lying at some distance from her bed, and that you called the neighbours at daybreak. Why did you not light a lamp as soon as you came and saw, and why did you not immediately call your neighbours instead of keeping quiet?

A.—I called out for my neighbours as soon as I saw my child on my return from the field.

Q.—Did you tell the *punchayet* of the village and the police at the *thanna* that your daughter had died of snake-bite?

A.—Yes, I said that my neighbours say that my child has died of snake-bite.

Q.—Will you call any witnesses?

A.—Yes, I will.

Q.—What will they say?

A.—They will say that they said about the snake-bite.

P. DICKENS,
Sessions Judge.

MEMO. OF THE STATEMENT OF THE ACCUSED.

My wife was away. I went to bed with my two little girls, Nekjan and Golak. Towards the end of the night I went to look after my onion field. · I found some cattle trespassing, and drove them away. I returned and smoked. When I came to my children I found that Nekjan's head had rolled off the pillow and was lying on the ground. I raised her up, and found she was dead. I began to lament loudly. My brother-in-law, Umesh Gazee, came. Afterwards came Sajan, Jameer, some women, and others. Then Umesh went to call Uma Charan, *punchayet.* We found a small wound on her belly, so big. [Shows on a piece of paper.] Uma Charan and others told me I was to go and inform at the *thanna.* I went towards the *thanna,* but was arrested by a *peon* on the road who had a warrant for me. He kept me about an' hour, and let me go on payment of 4 *annas.* I reached the *thanna* about 3 P.M. The wound was only skin-deep. When Ram Das, constable, came, he made me stretch out the wound, and it was then clear that it was not deep; it looked as if a piece of skin had been pinched out, and everyone said it was snake-bite.

(Sd.)   A. C. BRETT,
Judge.

July 24, 1882.

No witness is called for the defence.

(Sd.)   A. C. BRETT,
Judge.,

July 24, 1882.

At the close of the case for the prosecution, the Judge asked the Government Pleader to sum up his case.

The Government Pleader said he would rather not address the Jury, but would leave the case in the hands of the Court.

The Judge remarked that he saw no reason why the Government Pleader in this case wished to depart from the usual practice, and that it would be better for him to address the Court.

The Government Pleader then summed up the case for the prosecution. He saw no reason why the evidence of the witnesses for the prosecution, especially that of the prisoner's wife and daughter, should not be believed by the Jury.

Mr. Manomohan Ghose, in addressing the Jury on behalf of the prisoner, after some prefatory remarks, dwelt on the complete absence of any motive for the crime with which the prisoner was charged. Although, as matter of law, it was not incumbent on the prosecution to prove a motive for the crime, yet if ever there was a case in which the Jury would require the most satisfactory evidence of motive, it was the present, in which the prisoner was said to have murdered his own child, of whom he was admittedly very fond. The motive suggested by the prosecution—namely, that the prisoner intended to bring a false charge of murder against his enemies—was completely negatived by his own conduct immediately after the death of his daughter, when he never even suggested that his daughter had died by violence, much less been murdered by

Kadam Ali Fakir. A desperate attempt had been made by the prosecution, or some one who was pulling the strings from behind, to
supply the missing link on the present occasion, by making the child
Golak depose here for the first time that the prisoner, while committing the murder, had advised her to accuse the Fakir, but this piece
of evidence was manifestly tutored ; for, if true, the girl would undoubtedly have said so either at Bongong or in the Sessions Court at
Nuddea. In the High Court, while arguing the appeal of the prisoner, Mr. Ghose had pointed out the total absence of evidence of
motive, and had, as he now thought, somewhat injudiciously
observed that even the girl did not say that the prisoner had
advised her to accuse anyone else. When this argument was
used, nobody knew that the case would have to be re-tried, and the
girl's evidence on the present occasion seemed to have been prepared
for the express purpose of meeting this argument, which had been
previously urged in favour of the prisoner. On the medical evidence,
and especially from the fact that not a drop of blood ever came out
of the wound in the abdomen, the Jury would have no doubt whatever
that the wound in question was not the cause of death, but that it
was inflicted after death for some purpose or other, if it really had ever
attained the size which the doctor had described. The evidence of
the head-constable, corroborated by his entry, made at the time in
his inquest report, showed that the wound, when first seen, was a
small triangular wound ; the prisoner himself had described it as slight
before the police came, and it was obvious that the spear produced in
Court could not possibly have caused a triangular wound. It became,
therefore, necessary to say that the wound was not triangular; and accordingly the doctor, who was an intimate friend of the inspector,
had either given subsequently a description of the wound which was
not true, or the wound had been made to assume a different shape
before the body was examined by him. The *punchayet* witness had
also admitted that when he first saw the wound, it was as the head-
constable had described it in his report. It was most important to
bear in mind, as admitted by all the witnesses, that the villagers and

the police, when they first saw this wound, all thought it might have been snake-bite. There was then nothing in the size of the wound or in the appearance of the corpse inconsistent with the hypothesis of the child having died of snake-bite. The police and the villagers went the length of digging the floor of the prisoner's house for several hours in order to discover the snake. This fact had a most important bearing on the case, both as regards the size of the wound, as well as the prisoner's conduct; and this important fact had not, unfortunately, been elicited at Nuddea. Mr. Ghose also relied upon this fact for another purpose. During the previous trial at Nuddea, the police had tried to make out that the reason why the head-constable had not been able to examine the child Golak on Wednesday was that the prisoner had taken care to conceal her in the onion field during the whole time that the head-constable was in the village. This was the case for the prosecution at Nuddea ; and it was the case here also, as the Government Pleader had stated in his opening address. If the prosecution had succeeded in establishing this circumstance, it would undoubtedly have been most damaging to the prisoner; but Mr. Ghose had the satisfaction of feeling that he had completely succeeded in exposing the villainy which led to the concoction of this piece of evidence. Not only the child, in her examination-in-chief, had forgotten her instructions regarding her father having sent her away, but when taken unawares, and not perceiving the drift of the question, she readily admitted having been present on the Wednesday morning at the digging incident, which naturally had made an impression on her mind. She even pointed out the head-constable who superintended the digging in her presence, and admitted, in re-examination, that the corpse was then in the house, though she had stated in her examination-in-chief that she did not return from the onion field before the corpse was sent away. It was therefore clear that the police had deliberately fabricated this part of the case, partly to account for not examining the girl, and partly to prejudice the mind of the Court against the prisoner. This case showed how important it was for the Court in every case to send for the police papers and to test with the aid of those papers the evidence given in Court. As regards the evidence of the child (the only eye-witness in the case), Mr. Ghose remarked that no one who had heard her in Court could for a moment doubt that she had been tutored to tell a short story, and that her conduct was most unnatural, and unlike that of a simple truthful child. She first denied that her mother's mother was alive, and on being pressed said she could not answer the question without consulting her mother! This reply of the child was far more significant and impressive than if fifty witnesses had come forward to prove that she had been tutored. The Jury would be able to judge from this circumstance alone how utterly worthless the child's story was. This grandmother was in the house that night, and she would be the first person to whom the child would naturally report the matter, if she had really seen her sister being killed, and this grandmother's very existence even was at first denied by the child, who, on second thoughts, said she must consult her mother before answering any more questions about her grandmother. On points on which the child had not been instructed she came out with the truth like a child, but she was far too intelligent not to stick to the principal parts of her story. Mr. Ghose then commented in detail on the evidence of the prisoner's wife, and on her conduct, and characterised the other witnesses for the prosecution as utterly unworthy of credit, and brought up to support a false case, observing that it was perfectly clear that the deceased had never been killed by anyone; that she had died either a natural and sudden death, or had died from snake-bite. The wound on the abdomen, if not originally a bite, must have been fabricated after death. If fabricated on behalf of the prisoner, it must have been foolishly, and through fear, done for the purpose of manufacturing a snake-bite, after no bite was discovered on searching the body; and if fabricated by an enemy, it must have been done for the purpose of making evidence against the prisoner. The child might have been bitten by a snake on the head—and no one had examined her long hair to see if there was a bite—or she might have been bitten on some other part of the body. It was not necessary for the Jury to speculate as to how the child had died, nor was it incumbent on the prisoner to explain that. Any number of suggestions could be made as to the probable cause of the child's death, but such speculations were wholly unnecessary. It was enough for the prisoner to show that the medical evidence could not be relied upon ; that the child's story was a pure fabrication, and that she had been put up by the police and her mother to tell this story. The inspector, who had the getting up of the evidence, though present in Court, had not ventured to come forward to be cross-examined, or to deny the statements of the witnesses which affected him ; and the Jury could have no doubt that Dwarka Rai, constable, who had told a number of lies, and the inspector, who had not the courage to come forward, really knew more about the true history and the origin of this extraordinary case than either of them had thought it fit or safe to disclose. The prisoner had not been defended before, and many important facts had not, consequently, been elicited at the previous trial. This case showed the great danger of relying implicitly on the evidence of little children, and convicting persons on the strength of *post-mortem* reports made by incompetent doctors, after careless and perfunctory examination of the body. It also showed how necessary it was to cross-examine the witnesses carefully on points connected with the origin and the first inception of a case, as it was quite clear that for the first three days the witnesses never came out with their present story ; and it was not until Friday morning that the inspector got the prisoner's wife and child to accuse him. Mr. Ghose was therefore confident the Jury would acquit the prisoner without any hesitation.

THE JUDGE'S CHARGE TO THE JURY.

Gentlemen of the Jury,—The prisoner is charged with the murder of his own child, a little girl under 10 years of age—a child of whom he has been said to have been fond, and to whom he has been said to have been kind, and the only eye-witness is another child of his, a little girl younger than the deceased. To account for the prisoner's act (an act, the brutality of which renders it, I may say, incredible, unless accounted for by motive or explained by insanity), the prosecution says that the prisoner had a quarrel with one Kadam Ali Fakir, with whose wife he was suspected of having had criminal familiarity, and who had taken proceedings against him, and that he (the prisoner) killed his daughter in order to fasten a charge on his enemy, Kadam Ali.

It has been impossible to conceal from you during the trial of the case, that a Jury sitting at Nuddea had found the prisoner guilty of murder, and that sentence of death had been recorded against him. But, as has been very properly put to you by the Government Pleader, you must not allow that fact to influence you in any way, and you must approach the case as if it was an absolutely new one.

The manner in which the prisoner is said to have killed his child (Nekjan) is this : On Monday afternoon, the 27th March, prisoner sent his wife to his brother's house. She took with her one little girl and a sucking infant. Prisoner was left with two girls, Nekjan and Golak. They three went to sleep on the same mat in the verandah. In the night Golak was awakened by Nekjan kicking her, and when she opened her eyes she saw that her father was pressing Nekjan's throat with his foot, so that she (Nekjan) could not articulate, but was writhing, and then stabbed her with a spear in the abdomen. After this Nekjan lay still, and Golak knew by pulling her that she was dead.

Now, if a person is suffocated and stabbed, you expect to be told that a *post-mortem* examination of the body will enable a medical expert to tell us that he saw signs of suffocation, and that death was evidently produced either partly by suffocation and partly by stabbing (that is, by the combination of two injuries), or wholly by one or the other. But in this case we have the following extraordinary results from the medical evidence:—1. No trace of suffocation was observed by the doctor who cut up the body. 2. The wound of the abdomen, which that doctor reported after he had examined the body to be the cause of death, is not a serious wound. 3. The superior of that doctor, to whom his report was submitted, tells us that he does not think the materials are sufficient for us to predicate that the wound was inflicted during life or after death. 4. The superior officer tells us that he does not think the former had sufficient cause to state as a matter of certainty that death was not caused by srake-bite. 5. He also tells us that if the child had died from snake-bite in the abdomen, and that some one had shortly after death increased the size of the wound, the symptoms observed in the body would not be inconsistent with such a hypothesis. I must direct you that on such medical evidence, which was the only evidence submitted to you, it is impossible for you to find that Nekjan was killed by violence. You will remember a curious incident which came out in the examination of the native doctor, viz., that that officer, in column 3 of his report, writes that the wound was triangular, and he tells us that (though this was not proved) he had inserted this in his report, which he drew up after making his examination, because the police had reported it to be triangular. Again, though there were appearances in the body calculated to suggest the suspicion of strangulation, the native doctor made no examination specially calculated to elucidate the point. Further, though he observed that no blood seemed to have flowed out of the wound, he did not examine whether there was anything to show that circulation had been suspended previously to its infliction (which is the only possible cause which could prevent blood coming out), and he did not even notice the fact in his report. I regret to be compelled to say that the inference is that this officer conducted his *post-mortem* examination in a most perfunctory manner, and acted in a manner which shows that he did not realise the responsibilities of his position. Placed as he was in the position of a scientific expert, he gave expression to categorical opinions on insufficient data in a matter of life and death. Whilst I am on the subject of the wound, I would point out to you how extraordinary it is that the native doctor should state that it is such a wound as would be produced by a spear. When the prisoner went, on the

28th, to the *thanna*; he reported that his child had died from snake-bite, and that there was a *slight* wound on her stomach. Mark the word *slight*. The man must have known that a police officer would . be soon on the spot, and if the wound had been such as the native . doctor describes, his story would at once have been proved to be false. Again, when the head-constable came down (he was clearly not in a hurry, but acted as one would expect him to do when nothing grave was before him), he held the usual *suruth-hal*, or rough inquest, prevalent in the *mofussil*, and reported the wound to be slight and triangular in shape. You will remember the witness Uma Charan (a witness of whom I will have to speak later on); he is the village *punchayet*, and when he was in the witness-box I drew a triangle and a straight line on a piece of paper and asked him what was the shape of the wound. He selected the triangle. How, then, did the triangular wound of Tuesday become the rectilineal wound of Wednesday or Thursday? The whole of this portion of the case tends to lead one's mind into a path which might carry us to most startling conclusions, but which must pass through the mire of uncertainty; and in the present case it is specially necessary to divest your minds of all speculation, and keep steadily before you the affirmative issue—"Has the prosecution proved the prisoner's guilt?" But I have placed these considerations before you because they tend to emphasise the worthlessness of the native doctor's report.

But although we are left in the dark by the medical evidence, yet, if you believe the story told by the child Golak, there is sufficient for you to come to the conclusion that the prisoner killed Nekjan, and such killing would be murder. I will now proceed to examine the child's story, connecting it, of course, with the depositions of the other witnesses, and will simply premise this: It is, of course, necessary in every case to weigh carefully every statement, but if there is a case where more anxious deliberation than ordinary is called for, it would be such a one as the present, where the medical evidence does not help the statement of the witness.

Now, you have seen this little girl, and you will have noticed that she is intelligent. At the outset of her story we are met with a considerable discrepancy between what she says now and what she said before the Magistrate. Before the Magistrate she said she awoke to answer a call of nature, but here she says her sister kicked her. To the judge of Nuddea she said something touched her body. She says that what she told the Magistrate was a lapse of memory : you will remember the vernacular expression she employed. Apart from other considerations, this is a serious discrepancy ; but does it not raise in your minds a suspicion that some one has made the child give an account that would sound better than the first? Again, you will note—and this is of the highest importance—that in this Court she has added a statement of which not a word was breathed at Bongong or at Nuddea, namely, when she questioned her father at the time, he told her to lay the blame on the Fakir. The effect of this is, of course, to make a basis for the story of motive to which I have before alluded, and to which I will again refer. And the prisoner's wife, in answer to some questions which were put to her by myself, says that the child told her that her father had said to her—" The blame will be round the neck of Kadam Ali ". Now, do you consider that if the prisoner had really made any such statement, it would only come out at this stage? If he did not, the child must be lying in saying that he did ; and if she lies, she must have been taught to lie. Now, in connection with this, I will draw your attention to the following circumstances :—You will remember that this case commenced in this Court on Friday ; on that day were examined three witnesses, and on Saturday the first witness in the box was the child ; she was in attendance on Friday, and she was asked on Saturday what happened to her on Friday after she was released from attendance. She tells us that she and her mother were taken to the inspector's residence, and there she and her mother were introduced to him separately, and she was made to rehearse her story. Of course the inference is, from the child's evidence, that the mother was made to do the same. The mother denies this. You will weigh the statements. Again, you will note that the child was asked a very simple question as to whether her mother's mother was alive, and that, though she evinced a singular reluctance to answer this, she eventually admitted that she was alive (and there can be no doubt the old woman lives in the same premises); and once, when the question was pressed, she said, "I must ask my mother". It is inconceivable that a child should have any natural difficulty in saying that she had a maternal grandmother living in the same house, and thus you have before you the following facts :—(1) The child at the third hearing of the case introduces an entirely new feature about her father having told her to lay the blame on his enemy; (2) she tells us how she was taken, after leaving this Court, to rehearse her story to the inspector; (3) whilst questioned as to a circumstance, which must have been as well known to her as the alternation of day and night, she says she must ask her mother; and still further, you will remember that as a child she was not sworn as an adult, but she was questioned as to her knowledge of truth, and she said that a lie was a sin—*pâp* was the word she used, and that she told us the inspector had drilled her on this subject. You will have to say whether these circumstances lead you to accept the child as a spontaneous witness of what she saw, or as a witness who has learnt a lesson. And I need hardly point out to you that, just as a child's evidence is ordinarily valuable, because of its *primâ facie* spontaneity, so is its value depreciated when there is anything to cause a suspicion of tutoring, because of the facility with which children yield to outside influence.

Then look at the manner in which the case is presented to us. The person to put the engine in motion is the prisoner. He told the police that there was a slight wound on his child's stomach, and that he thought she had been bitten by a snake. The head-constable, Ram Das, evidently thought that there was nothing calling for a display of energy, and sent his subordinate, Dwarka Rai. This man was treated by the prosecution as a merely formal witness, who had to prove the identity of the corpse. But when he was subjected to cross-examination, he turned out to be a thoroughly unsatisfactory witness, who, though he was deputed by the inspector to take a leading part in the investigation, and must have known as much, and perhaps more, than anyone connected with the case, sheltered himself under the plea of "I do not remember," almost invariably, whenever any important question was asked him, and whose evidence was so full of contradictions that it was difficult to record. When the inspector was told by the native doctor that the case was one of murder, this man was the official selected to go down and see into it. He tells us that he did not ask the prisoner's wife and child what they knew. This is a statement in itself difficult to believe, and it is directly contradicted by the wife, who says that the first person to whom she told what she knew was this Dwarka.

I have said that Ram Das was not in a hurry. After sending Dwarka on Tuesday, he followed on Wednesday. I have already told you how he accepted the theory of snake-bite, held his inquest, and reported accordingly. Whatever you may think of his subsequent conduct, there is nothing to show he was not then acting with *bonâ fides.* He tells us that he very carefully examined the wound on the abdomen, and that it was superficial and triangular. He also tells us that he asked prisoner's wife what she knew, and that she said—"I was not there. I cannot say how the child died." He tells us that the floor of prisoner's verandah was dug up, and a search was made for a snake. You will have noted how the other witnesses have answered questions as to this digging up, and you will consider whether you are satisfied that the floor was dug up. You will ask yourselves whether you do or do not think that there was then a *bonâ fide* belief in the theory of snake-bite. On this point you will notice that the man Umesh Ghazee, who is said to have dug up the floor, is not called by the prosecution, and his wife Dhiru, who is called, says he took a *kodali* (spade) for the purpose of digging up the floor.

The next stage in the case is, that the body is examined by the native doctor, whose report I have already analysed for your benefit. I need not recapitulate. The result was that the prisoner was put on his trial for murder.

Now the men who took up the clue given by the doctor were Dwarka, constable (under the orders of the inspector), and the inspector himself. I have examined the *non me recordo* evidence of Dwarka, and it is certainly a singular fact that the inspector has not been put into the witness-box, and this point I would draw your attention to. ‹ Assuming that the native doctor found a deep incised wound, the only thing 'that he could predicate was that it had been caused by a sharp-cutting instrument. But Dwarka tells us that the inspector ordered him to go and look for a spear.

It is clear that a number of men were on the spot soon after the event, and yet the only man produced is Uma Charan Punchayet. The prosecutor says that the first person to come to the prisoner's house after the murder was the old woman Haru, and the next was the younger Dhiru, sister of prisoner's wife. You will notice that although these women are supposed to have been attracted by the cries of a child, yet the child says she never cried ; and in fact, part of the evidence goes to show that it was the prisoner who raised the lamentation which drew the attention of the neighbourhood. The child says that her father, when he returned, called out loudly—" Oh, neighbours, how is it my Nekjan is dead ? " Although the wife told the Judge of Nuddea that she found her husband crying, she says here most emphatically that he never cried. *e*

The old woman Haru's statement is as follows :—She says she heard the child crying, and went to her, and then found the prisoner with the living child and the corpse. Golak told her that her father had killed Nekjan in the manner related, and the prisoner lifted his hand on the child in a threatening manner, but did not strike her. She contradicts here what she said at Nuddea on two points. There‹ she said she saw a wound : here she says she did not. There she said prisoner threatened to strangle Golak : here she says he did not. From the evidence of Dhiru (sister of prisoner's wife), whether she went to prisoner's house or not, it is clear that her husband preceded her, and, as I have pointed out before, though he must be a material witness, he is not called. This woman says she did not go up to the body, and she is throughout consistent in what she says the child told her, which is, that the prisoner had killed Nekjan by pressing her throat with his foot, but without mentioning anything about the spear. The prisoner's wife is the next woman brought on the stage, and she says that the prisoner's guilt was revealed to her by the child. It is manifest that the object of the prosecution in tendering these three women for examination as witnesses is to get over or avoid the stumbling-block created by the inference that the child had not said to those around her what she had seen. The case for the prosecution now is, that she told it to Haru at one time, to Dhiru at another, and to her own mother at another. No two together, you observe. Sporadic evidence of this description is easy to make, and presents few opportunities to the cross-examiner. And it seems to me to raise another difficulty whilst endeavouring to avoid the first. Prisoner's wife knew the facts when Dwarka came first, and when Ram Das followed him. She admits hearing her husband tell the police that the child had died from snake-bite. She narrates to us vividly the particulars of a violent quarrel she had with her husband when she discovered and noted the perfidy with which he had sent her out of the way. She told him she would never give him his rice again, and he told her he would never again take it at her hands. You, gentlemen, will understand that this was war to the knife declared between them. But she says she never said a word to any policeman till Dwarka's second visit, and her explanation is that she was not called. She is contradicted by Ram Das, who says that he did ask her what she knew, and she is contradicted by Dwarka, who says he did not ask her, and her name is attached to the report of the inquest sent in by Ram Das.

I have previously drawn your attention to the fact that, of all the men of the village who must have known something of the facts, only one has been called. The exception is Uma Charan Punchayet. This man commences his evidence by saying that Umesh Ghazee (you will remember him as the husband of Dhiru and the man who dug the floor, but has not been called) came to him and told him that he was requested to come by the prisoner and a number of men, as Nekjan was lying dead. He went and saw the corpse, asked the prisoner how the child had died, and was told by him at first that he could not tell, and afterwards that it was a snake-bite. He examined the body, and saw a *triangular* wound. The rest of his evidence is an attempt to make us believe that he had his suspicion; that he saw a spear in some jungle in one place and a large sacrificial knife in another place; that he gave orders that these were not to be touched, and he told the prisoner to go and report the matter to the police, and to take a written report with him, which he (witness) was just going to write at his own house; that the prisoner never came, and the report was never written. The counsel for the prisoner has described this in addressing you as a "cock-and-bull" story. The epithet is a graphic one, and I think appropriate. And we find that this man's name is attached to the report of the inquest. Ram Das was examined after Uma Charan, and it was during the examination of Ram Das that this fact was discovered; otherwise, probably, Uma Charan would have been severely cross-examined on the point.

I have already told you that there is no legal necessity for the prosecution to prove the existence of a motive for the deed. But the prosecution has very naturally considered it advisable to set up and try to prove a motive. But up to the time the case was presented in this Court, the existence of the motive was a matter of pure specu-lation. Certainly, the prisoner had been accused by one Kadam Ali Fakir of having indecently assaulted his wife; and after hearing the woman, who has been put into the witness-box before us, we may reasonably entertain a strong suspicion that there was an intrigue between her and the prisoner. But there was nothing but hypothesis on which to construct the theory of motive, and when the obvious objection was raised that the prisoner had made no accusation against the Fakir, the prosecution was driven to another hypothesis, and that was, that probably the prisoner had changed his mind, and feared to go on when he found that his other child had blurted out the truth.

This is not evidence; it is imagination. Now, as I have said, we have the child saying that her father disclosed his plot to her at the time. That is to say, what was before based on nothing is now based on a lie!

, It has been argued—"Can you believe that a child and a wife can try and bring a man to the scaffold by giving false evidence?" No doubt, it is a violent shock to one's feelings to suppose so. But a very suggestive circumstance has been deposed to in this Court by the child. She says that after her father was sentenced to death at Nuddea, her mother made an offering at the foot of a sacred tree near the Court, and gave her some of the sweetmeats which she had offered. The mother denies this. You have heard them both, and you will say which you believe. Further, the woman admits that she never went to see her husband in prison, and that though persons in Court told her that she could appeal for nothing, she made no attempt to do so. If you infer from these circumstances the existence of an animus on the part of the wife, not only does the difficulty disappear, but you can readily understand how easily the mother, and through her the child, could be manipulated.

You have, then—(1) Medical evidence founded on a perfunctory *post-mortem* and a self-contradictory report, which leaves the question of the cause of death unsolved ; (2) the deposition of the child, eye-witness, with a manifest lie in it, and open to very grave suspicion of having been tutored; (3) the general evidence, which I have analysed for you; (4) the story of the motive, originally pure speculation, requiring additional speculation to make it plausible, and now supported by a lie ; and (5) the evidence as to animus on the part of the wife. No doubt the case is involved in mystery ; but your duty does not extend to the discovery of absolute truth, but only to discovering whether it is proved that the prisoner is guilty.

July 24, 1882. (Sd.) A. C. BRETT.

The jury, after retiring for less than a minute, returned a unanimous verdict of "Not guilty," in which the Judge said he entirely concurred. The prisoner was thereupon acquitted and released.

CHAPTER V.

THE MYSTERY REVEALED.

AFTER the case was transferred by the High Court from Nuddea to Alipur for re-trial, I decided to defend the prisoner, and about the middle of July, 1882, I visited him in the Nuddea jail, at the request of his Pleader, Baboo Akhay Kumar Mukerjee, who thought that if I personally saw the prisoner, he might be disposed to communicate to me some information regarding the case likely to prove useful at the second trial. I was accompanied by the Pleader and by Dr. Brander, the superintendent of the jail, who stated to me that from the beginning he had entertained grave doubts regarding the prisoner's guilt, and who also expressed his regret that during the trial at Nuddea there was no one to examine him on behalf of the prisoner, and to elicit from him evidence likely to help the defence. Soon after our arrival, the prisoner was brought in, and on my name being mentioned to him he fell prostrate at my feet and began to weep. What transpired at the interview will appear from the following conversation between the prisoner and myself:—

"I am entirely innocent. Save my life."

"But how did your child die? Until you are able to give me some information on this point, it will not be possible for any of us to defend you properly."

"I know nothing about it."

"You must know something, and unless you tell us the truth on this point we can do nothing; your case is an extremely difficult one."

"I know nothing."

"But why does your own daughter accuse you of the murder?"

"The police have tutored her, and her statements are false. My wife and daughter have both been saying what they were taught to say."

At this stage Dr. Brander and the Pleader left the room at my request, and the conversation between the prisoner and myself proceeded :—

"I am quite convinced in my own mind that you know how your child died, and unless you explain to me the cause of the child's death, I shall find it extremly difficult to defend you at the trial."

"I found my child dead on my return from the field. I don't know how she died. Do as you like, but I know nothing."

"Muluk Chand! I believe you did not intentionally kill your child; but I cannot believe you know nothing. If you decline to tell me the truth, you make it almost impossible for me to defend you, and you run the risk of being hanged."

"I know nothing."

"Never mind how your child was killed. I am certain that the wound on her body was inflicted after death, and you must know all about it."

[At this the prisoner looked confused and agitated, and caught hold of my feet.]

"What makes you say the wound was caused after death?"

"I am sure it was."

"Have you heard it from Umesh Ghazee, my brother-in-law?"

"I never heard of him. But what does he know?"

"Well, sir, as you know all about the wound, if you will excuse me, I will tell you everything. That man, Umesh Ghazee, is the cause of all my troubles. He made the wound, and advised me to say that it was a snake-bite. When we discovered that my child Nekjan was dead, and did not know how to account for her death, my brother-in-law, Umesh Ghazee, brought his small knife and made the wound, but no blood came out of it, as the child was then dead."

" What about the spear ? Was that never used ?"

" No, the spear was never thought of until the police got my child to accuse me of murder."

" Did not your child accuse you when your wife returned home and before the police came ?"

" All that is utterly untrue. I was not accused before Thursday night. When Ram Das Jemadar came on Wednesday, he made Umesh Ghazee dig the floor of my house in the hope of getting the snake. My child, Golak, was there then, and so was my wife. The inspector subsequently sent for my wife and child, and told them I had myself confessed, and got them to say what he liked. I met my wife one day, as I was being taken to the Magistrate's Court, and she cried out—' Is it true you have admitted having killed Nekjan ?' I replied—' No, it is all false '."

I then said—" I am glad you have told me all about the wound. But why did Umesh Ghazee make it so big ?"

" It was very slight at first, but it was subsequently enlarged by the police while the corpse was being carried to Bongong. They wanted Rs. 30 from me, but I had not so much to give them."

It will thus be seen that when I defended the accused at Alipur, at the second trial, I had no information whatever regarding the cause of the child's death, but I felt convinced in my own mind that the case was not one of murder, and that the prisoner probably had not ventured to disclose the whole truth. I was, however, greatly relieved to find that I had elicited during the interview one most valuable piece of information, which showed that the theory I had put forward before the High Court was perfectly correct, viz., that the wound on the deceased child had been fabricated after death. This fact once established, the conclusion became irresistible that the medical evidence in the case could not be depended upon, as it could throw no light whatever on the cause of the child's death. The information regarding the digging of the floor by Umesh

Ghazee, under the orders of the police, appeared to be of the utmost importance, as nothing had transpired regarding this matter at the first trial. The fact that at the second trial Umesh Ghazee's wife, Dhiru, fainted, or pretended to faint, when cross-examined about the part her own husband had played in the case, was full of significance to those who knew the secret at the time ; but to the Judge, the Jury, and to the public at large her conduct in the witness-box seemed to have no special meaning.*

On the morning of the 25th July, 1882, the day after the acquittal of Muluk Chand Chaukidar, his daughter, Golak Mani, accompanied by her mother, came to see him in my house, and I had then the following conversation with the child :—

" Who killed your sister ? "

No answer.

Question repeated.

The girl, with tears in her eyes—" I don't know ".

" Did you not see your father kill her ? "

" No. I was asleep ; and I know nothing."

" But you said in Court only the other day that you saw your father kill her ? "

The child, crying—" I was taught to say that ".

" Who taught you ? "

" Dwarik Constable showed me a sword, and said—' If you do not say that your father killed your sister with his spear, I will cut off your head with this sword ; but if you say that in Court, your father will be released and will come home'; I therefore agreed to say that."

" But what made you say that, even after you heard that your father was going to be hanged ? "

" My mother and the *daroga* (police inspector) said I must say what I had said before, or else I should be punished."

The mother of the child, who was standing by, remained silent the whole time, and did not answer a single question put to her. She looked sad and in great distress of mind.

* Page 64.

A few days after the acquittal of Muluk Chand I sent for him with a view to ascertain, if possible, the true cause of Nekjan's death; and on that occasion the following conversation took place between him and me :—

" Muluk Chand, you know that you are acquitted, and that even if you are guilty you cannot now be punished. You have nothing to fear. Tell me truly how your child died."

Muluk Chand, with tears in his eyes, catching hold of my feet— "You have saved my life, and I would not deceive you on any account. I am the most miserable creature on earth, and I ought to have been hanged. It would have been better for me."

"What ! Did you, then, kill your child ? "

"You have every right to call me the murderer of my daughter, though I would have gladly given my own life to save hers."

"Tell me the whole truth without any fear."

Muluk Chand then, with tears in his eyes, made the following statement to me :—

" On Monday night I was sleeping in my verandah with my two daughters. My wife had gone away to bring some money from my brother. I have some vegetables growing in my yard below my verandah, and opposite to it is my cowshed, where I keep a cow. There was a stray bull in our village which gave me much trouble. It used to come almost every night to my house and cause mischief. In order to drive the animal away, I used to keep near my pillow a *khatia* (the pole of a husking machine, a heavy piece of wood about a yard in length, and about 14 to 18 inches in circumference), and whenever the animal came, I used to run after it with that *khatia*. On Monday night it was dark and cloudy, and I fancy it was about 2 A.M. when I heard, while sleeping, some footsteps which I imagined to be those of the bull, just below my verandah and opposite the cowshed. Believing the animal had come again, and without going up to it, I threw my *khatia* with great force towards the spot where I imagined the bull was standing. I immediately heard the sound, 'Oh ma !' and recognising the voice of my darling child [*Bachha* was the word used], I felt convinced that she had been hit. She had quietly gone down in the dark without my knowledge, probably to answer some call of nature. I at once rushed out and lifted her up in my arms, but found she was gasping and unable to speak. The *khatia* had hit her on the back, just below the neck, but the mark of the blow was not noticed by the police and the villagers.* I lighted a lamp and saw that my child was dead, and that blood was coming out of her mouth and nostrils. My first impulse was to throw myself into a well or the river and commit suicide, and with that intention I went a few paces ; but I changed my mind and thought I had better consult my brother-in-law, Umesh Ghazee, who was sleeping in an adjoining house. I called him and told him what had happened. He said—' What have you done ? The police will come to-morrow morning, tie your hands and get you imprisoned for ten years.' I asked his advice, and he first suggested that I should give out that the bull had killed the child, but I declined to accept that suggestion, as I knew that some men of our village in a recent case had set up the defence that a young man who had complained of certain injuries had been gored by a bull, but this defence was not believed, and the accused were convicted. Umesh Ghazee then suggested that I might accuse the Fakirs who were at enmity with me, but this I declined to do. He then said—' Your best plan is to say that your daughter died of snake-bite'. To which I replied—' But there is no mark of any bite'. ' That is easily done,' said he ; ' let me go and fetch my small knife with which I cut mangoes, and let us make a bite.' Saying this, he went to his room and brought his knife, and said—' You make a snake-bite with this'. I said—' I will not lay violent hands on my dead child ; you do as you think best '. Thereupon Umesh Ghazee made a

* It will be seen that the doctor who made the *post-mortem* examination had not thought it necessary to examine the spinal cord of the deceased (see his cross-examination at the second trial, page 55). At the time the doctor was cross-examined I had no information whatever regarding any injury to the spinal cord, but the signs of death from asphyxia suggested the question to me. I may add that the accused was too ignorant to understand or to follow the medical evidence, which was given in English.—M. G.

slight wound in the abdomen. I asked—'Why have you selected that part of the body?' He replied—'If the snake had bitten the child in the foot or in the hand, how is it she did not wake up? But if she was bitten in the abdomen, she must have become unconscious instantly.'* He then said—'Now go in the direction of your onion field, and on your return, after a while, call us all and say that your child has died of snake-bite'. I acted according to this advice, and roused all my neighbours, early on Tuesday morning. They all came and examined the body, and imagined Nekjan had died of snake-bite. I left for the *thanna* (police station) before my wife returned, and met there Inspector Golam Rahman, who knew me well, and had been very kind to me. I told him privately that I had come to report the death of my child; that I did not know how she died at night; and that some of my neighbours said she died of snake-bite, while others said my enemies, the Fakirs, might have killed her. He then advised me on no account to accuse anyone, but simply to state that I did not know how the child died. He said he was about to go away on leave that day; but he would direct his head-constable to be kind to me. He then sent for Ram Das Sircar, head-constable, and said—'Go and see this man's child, and be kind to him. Don't take any money from him. I know he is poor. Go and inquire how his child died, and if it is a case of snake-bite, report accordingly.'

" After recording my statement, the head-constable left the station, but Dwarik Constable preceded him, and the head-constable came the next morning (Wednesday). After causing my floor to be dug up and examining my neighbours, the head-constable sent the corpse in charge of Dwarik Constable and some villagers, and I went with them. Before starting, Sham Mehtar and other neighbours told me that if I gave a few rupees to the police there would be no further trouble. I offered Rs. 6, but the police wanted Rs. 30. At last I borrowed Rs. 16, which Sham Mehtar took from me to give the

* It is popularly believed that a snake-bite in a vital part of the body caus instant insensibility.—M. G.

police. When taking the corpse to Bongong, we halted on the banks of the Ichamati at a place called Potkhali, where Dwarik Constable told me—'You *sala*,* pay for our breakfast; you have given me nothing, and unless you pay, you will get into trouble'. I said I had already paid Rs. 16. Dwarik said he had not got it, and that I must go and get some money. From Potkhali I went back ,and brought a couple of rupees. On my return, I saw the constable sitting by the side of the corpse examining the wound, which I saw had increased in size. I asked—'Who has done this?' The ferryman who was there said that the constable had been inserting the stump of an indigo plant into the wound. On hearing this, the constable got angry and threatened to beat the ferryman, saying—'*Sala*, can you say you have seen me do it?' The ferryman got frightened and said he had not seen it.

"After the examination of the body by the doctor, the police arrested me at Bongong, and sent for my wife and daughter. In the lock-up at night, I was beaten by the constables and told to confess. They brought date thorns and pierced them into the quick of my nails [showing four or five fingers with nails injured]. The inspector, accompanied by another *daroga* whom I don't know, came and said —'You better confess. Your daughter and wife are accusing you.' In spite of the torture, I declined to say anything. The constables then said—'If you did not do it, why do you not accuse Kadam Ali Fakir?' I declined to accuse him."

Q.—"What made you conceal the truth at the beginning? If you had come out with the truth at once, nothing would have happened to you."

A.—"I am an ignorant man, and I thought no one would believe me, and that the police would accuse me of murder even if I told the truth."

Q.—"But what made you conceal all this when I pressed you in the jail to tell me the truth?"

A.—"I then thought you would decline to defend me if I told

* A term of abuse.

the truth. Sir, I ask your forgiveness for it." [Saying this, he began to weep.]

Q.—"How do you account for the conduct of your wife? Is there any reason why she should have wished to get you hanged?"

A.—"I have no reason to suspect that she is unfaithful to me, but she was very jealous, and suspected me of undue familiarity with the wife of Kadam Ali Fakir. On returning home and finding the child dead, she said to me—'I know you want to live with the Fakir's wife, and that is why you have done this. I will not give you rice any more.' I said—'I shall not have to eat rice cooked by you any more'."

Q.—"Did you tell her on her return what had happened?"

A.—I told no one except Umesh Ghazee. He might have told his wife Dhiru. My daughter Golak was asleep till daylight and saw nothing. Dhiru, Haru, and my wife all gave false evidence through fear of the police."

Q.—"Can you explain the conduct of your wife in offering *shirni* * when you were sentenced to death?"

A—"The villagers all told her that she herself would get into trouble if the charge against me failed, and she says the offering was by Kadam Ali Fakir, at whose request she joined in it."

M. GHOSE.

* Sweets offered by way of thanks.

THE ABERDEEN UNIVERSITY PRESS.

www.ingramcontent.com/pod-product-compliance
Lightning Source LLC
Chambersburg PA
CBHW031929060726
47496CB00008BA/2613